NORSE MYTHOLOGY

Great Stories from the Eddas

Hamilton Wright Mabie

DOVER PUBLICATIONS, INC.
Mineola, New York

Dedication

To J. T. M.

Published in Canada by General Publishing Company, Ltd., 895 Don Mills Road, 400-2 Park Centre, Toronto, Ontario M3C 1W3.

Published in the United Kingdom by David & Charles, Brunel House, Forde Close, Newton Abbot, Devon, TQ12 4PU.

Bibliographical Note

Norse Mythology: Great Stories from the Eddas, first published in 2002, is an unabridged republication of the work originally published in 1918 by Dodd, Mead and Company, New York under the title *Norse Stories Retold from the Eddas.*

Library of Congress Cataloging-in-Publication Data

Mabie, Hamilton Wright, 1846–1916.
[Norse stories retold from the Eddas.]
Norse mythology : great stories from the Eddas / Hamilton Wright Mabie.
p. cm.
Summary: A collection of stories told by the Norsemen that "tell of the birth of the world and the coming of the gods to rule over them."
ISBN 0-486-42082-5 (pbk.)
1. Mythology, Norse—Juvenile literature. [1. Mythology, Norse.] I. Title.

BL860 .M235 2002
398.2'089'395—dc21

2001055264

Manufactured in the United States of America
Dover Publications, Inc., 31 East 2nd Street, Mineola, N.Y. 11501

Contents

I. The Making of the World

Eight hundred years ago, when the galleys of the bold Norsemen were scudding through storm and mist far into the unknown western seas, or, in the soft summer of the Mediterranean, riding at anchor in the ports of Italy and Northern Africa, the old stories of the battles of the gods and the giants that had been repeated for hundreds of years by Norse firesides in the long winter evening were brought together by some unknown man in Iceland, and were known henceforth as the Elder Edda; and a hundred years later Snorre Sturleson retold the same old stories, with others equally marvellous, in the Younger Edda. These ancient books, which a brave and noble race carried in its heart through all its wide wanderings and conquests, take one back to the beginning of time, and tell of the birth of the worlds and the coming of the gods to rule over them.

Norway faces the sea with a line of cliffs so massive that their foundations seem everlasting. Islands without number rise out of the tossing waves; the deep, tranquil waters of the fjords, overhung with fir-covered mountains, and bright at night with the quenchless splendour of the stars, flow through narrow channels to the outer ocean; and against the sky great mountains stand vast and immovable, as if from eternity to eternity. No Norseman, steering his adventurous galley along these rocky shores, seeing, perhaps, the mighty rush of the polar seas against the North Cape, and hearing the long reverberation of Thor's hammer roll from mountain peak to mountain peak, would have believed that these things had not been as he saw them from the very beginning, if the Eddas, wiser than any wisdom of man, had not told him of a time when even the gods had not begun to live, and in the vast space where no worlds hung and no heavens shone there was nothing but the unseen spirit of the great All-Father, solitary and silent in the depths.

Not even the Eddas are able to reveal his thoughts or to describe his life in the awful solitariness of a silent universe; they can only declare that in his own good time he began to build the worlds, and far in the north Niflheim rose out of the depths, the land of eternal winter wrapped in fogs and mists, and far in the south Muspelheim, the land of quenchless fire, glowing with unspeakable heat and overhung with clouds and fiery sparks, in the midst of whose blinding heat and light sat Surt, guarding the kingdom of fire with a flaming sword. Between the land of ice and the land of fire yawned the bottomless abyss, Ginungagap, black and fathomless, and into it the rivers of Niflheim poured with soundless fury, and as the icy streams fell into the darkness they congealed and hung in great masses from the northern edges of the abyss; and over the awful chasm and the silent cataracts icy fogs gathered and bitter winds swept.

Against the whirling snows and shifting fogs of Niflheim glowed the wandering flames and floating fires of Muspelheim, throwing broad beams of light far into the sunless abyss, and sending a wide glow through the drifting snow. Glittering sparks shot into the silent space above and floated far off towards the north like stars that had wandered from their courses; and as the icy mist met the burning heat in the upper air, it hung motionless for a brief moment and then fell drop by drop into the abyss, and there, out of heat and cold, fire and fog, in darkness and solitude, the giant Ymer grew into life. To give him food the cow Audhumbla was made, and as she stood nourishing the giant with her milk, she licked the icy stones which were covered with salt, and straightway the head of a man began to take shape, grew larger, and on the third day the man stood upright, fair of face and mighty of stature; and his name was Bure. Now Bure had a son, whom he called Bor, and Bor, in turn, became the father of Odin, Vile, and Ve, the first of the gods. The giant Ymer also was the father of many children who were frost-giants and enemies of the gods.

Ymer grew to such vast size, and was so full of evil, that Odin, Vile, and Ve could not live in peace with him, and at last they fell upon him, and slew him, and the blood poured in such torrents from his great body that all the giants, save Bergelmer and his wife, were drowned; these two alone escaped on a chest, and from them the whole race of the frost-giants sprang. The gods dragged Ymer's body into the centre of the abyss, and there they fashioned the world out of it. They wrought with divine beauty and power, spreading out the great plains, cutting the deep valleys through the hills, filling the wide seas and sending the waters far up into the deep fjords; and over all they stretched the bending heaven, and north, south, east, and west set a dwarf to keep it in place; and they caught the great sparks that floated out of Muspelheim and set them in the sky, until the splendour of the stars shone over the whole earth. Around the world lay the deep sea, an endless circle of waters, and beyond it were the dreary shores of Jotunheim, the home of the frost-giants.

To the giantess Night, and to her beautiful son Day, whose father was of their own number, the gods gave chariots and swift horses that they might ride through the sky once in every twenty-four hours. Night drove first behind the fleet Hrimfaxe, and as she ended her course at dawn bedewed the waiting earth with drops from his bit; Day flew swiftly after his dusky mother, the shining mane of his horse, Skinfaxe, filling the heavens with light. There was also one Mundilfare, who had a son and daughter of such exceeding beauty that he called the one Maane, or Moon, and the other Sol, or Sun; and the gods were so angry at his daring that they set the one to guide the Sun and the other the Moon in their daily courses around the world. So day and night, summer and winter, seed-time and harvest, were established.

In the very centre of the earth rose a lofty mountain, and on the top of it was the beautiful plain of Ida, overlooking all lands and seas. Here the gods came when their work was done, and looked upon all that they had made and saw that it was fair; the earth, green and fruitful, blossomed at their feet, and the heavens bent over them radiant with sun by day and filled with the soft splendour of moon and stars by night. And they chose the plain of Ida for their home, and built the shining city of Asgard. In the midst of it stood a hall of pure gold, whose walls were circled with the thrones of the twelve gods, and they called it Gladsheim. There was a noble hall for the goddesses also, and homes for all the gods. They made ready a great smithy, and filled it with all manner of tools, anvils, hammers, and tongs, with which to forge the weapons that were to slay the giants and keep the world in order. From earth to heaven they stretched Bifrost, the rainbow bridge, over which they passed and repassed in their journeyings.

When the work was done, and Asgard shone like a beautiful cloud overhanging the world, there came a time so peaceful and happy that it was called the Age of Gold. The gods had endless sport in games of skill and strength on the plains of Ida, and day and night the fires blazed in the smithy, as, with wonderful skill, they fashioned all kinds of curious things. There was no care nor sorrow anywhere; no clouds darkened the sun, no blights fell on the growing fields, no mighty tasks pressed on the hearts of the gods summoning them out of ease and pleasure to great enterprises and awful perils. At last the happy time came to an end, for one day the Norns, or fates, the three terrible sisters, Urd, Verdande, and Skuld, who determined the course of events and shaped the lives of things, took their abode at the foot of the tree Ygdrasil, and henceforth not even the gods were free from care.

The earth was fruitful, but no one tilled its field or crossed its seas; the shouts of children at play and the ringing voices of the reapers and harvesters were never heard. So the gods took the earth-mould and out of it they made the dwarfs and set them to work in the veins of metal and in dark caverns under ground. It happened also one day that Odin, Hoener, and Loder were walking together along the shore of the sea, and they came upon an ash and an elm, two beautiful trees, straight and symmetrical and crowned with foliage. Odin looked at them long, and a great thought came into his mind.

"Out of these trees," he said at last, "let us make man to fill the earth and make it fruitful, and he shall be our child, and we will care for him."

And out of the ash and the elm the first man and woman were made, and the gods called the man Ask and the woman Embla.

II. Gods and Men

A great many hundreds of years after the creation of the world, there ruled in Sweden a wise king whose name was Gylfe; and the wisdom of this king, like all wisdom, was in part knowledge and in larger part goodness. He knew how to give as well as how to receive. A wayfaring woman once found shelter at his hands, and, in return told him many wonderful stories; which so pleased the king that he gave her, as a reward, as much land as four oxen could plough in a day and a night. Now this woman was of the race of the gods and her name was Gefjun. She took four great oxen from Jotunheim, who were the offspring of a giant, and set them before the plough and drove them forth into the land which the king had set apart for her. And the plough, being drawn by giants, cut so deep into the soil, that it tore away a great piece of land, and carried it into the sea to the west, and there left it. Gefjun called this new country which she had taken from the mainland, Seeland; and the place from which the land was taken was filled by the sea and formed a lake which is now called Logrinn.

This was but the beginning of King Gylfe's acquaintance with the gods; for he was a seeker after wisdom and he who searches for wisdom must go to the gods to find it. He saw the wonderful things which the gods did and the marvellous ways in which their will was done in Asgard, and upon the earth, and he thought much upon their power and wondered whence it came. He could not make up his mind whether these gods, of whom he had heard and whose mighty works he saw, were powerful by reason of the force in themselves, or whether they were made strong by other and greater gods. After thinking much about these things and finding that no man could answer the questions which he was continually asking himself, Gylfe assumed the form of a very old man and made the long journey to Asgard, thinking to learn the secrets of the gods without letting them know who he was.

The gods know all things, and they not only knew that the old man who one day came to Asgard was Gylfe, but they knew that he was to make the journey long before he had so much as thought of it. They received him, however, as if they thought he was what he appeared to be, and he learned as much as he could understand; which is as much as a man ever learns.

The gods have often visited men, but men have rarely visited the gods, and the King's coming to Asgard was the beginning of a new wisdom among men.

No sooner did he enter the home of the gods than he found himself in a great hall, so high that he would hardly see over it. And the roof of this hall was thatched with shields of gold in place of shingles:

Thinking thatchers
Thatched the roof;
The beams of the burg
Beamed with gold.

When Gylfe came to the door of this great hall he saw a man playing with swords with such wonderful quickness and skill that he kept seven flashing in the air at one time. When this player with swords asked his name, the king speaking as an old man, answered that he was Ganglere, or the Walker, that he had come a long distance and that he begged a lodging for the night; and he asked, as if it were a very unimportant matter, who owned the hall. The man, who was a god in disguise, replied that it belonged to their king and that he would take Ganglere to him.

"You may ask him his name yourself when you see him," he added.

Then the man led the way into the hall and no sooner were they within its walls than the doors were shut. There were many rooms under the shining roof and every room seemed to be full of people, some of whom were playing games, and some were drinking out of great horns or cups, and some were fighting with different kinds of weapons; and Gylfe did not understand half of the things he saw. He was not at all frightened by his ignorance, however, and he said to himself:

> Gates all,
> Before in you go,
> You must examine well;
> For you cannot know
> Where enemies sit
> In the house before you.

When Gylfe had looked about him he saw three seats or thrones and upon each of these a man sat high above the throng which played and drank and fought.

"What are the names of these kings?" he asked. And the man who led him into the hall answered that he who sat on the lowest of the three thrones was the king and was called Har, and that he who sat on the throne next above him was called Jafnhar, and he who sat on the highest throne was called Thride. Now these three gods were as many different forms of Odin, and Gylfe was really seeing one god when he seemed to be seeing three.

Then Har, or Odin, spoke in a deep and wonderful tone and asked Gylfe who he was, and why he had come there, and bade him welcome by inviting him to eat and drink as much and often as he chose. But Gylfe was so bent upon learning the secrets of the gods that he did not think of food or drink, nor did he stop to answer Har's questions. He replied boldly that he wanted to find a wise man if there were one. Then Har answered him, as the gods often answer men, in words which were so full of meaning that he did not understand them until long afterwards:

"You shall not go from this place unharmed unless you go wiser than you came."

It is dangerous to seek the gods, unless we profit by what they tell us; for it is better to be ignorant than to possess knowledge and not live by it.

Then Gylfe stood boldly before Odin,—a man standing in the

presence of God and seeking for knowledge,—and asked many and deep questions about the gods and their ways and power; and about the giants, and their homes; and about the making of the world and the creation of man; and about the sun and moon and stars; and about the seasons and the wind and fire. And Odin answered his questions and told him the things which men are eager to know, but cannot learn unless the gods teach them.

When Odin had told Gylfe all that a man could understand of these deep mysteries he refused to answer any more questions and bade the questioner make the best use of what had been told him, and when Odin had spoken these words Gylfe heard a great noise and found himself standing alone in a great plain, and the hall and Asgard had vanished utterly. Then, filled with wonder by all he had heard and seen, he went home to his own kingdom, and told of the marvellous things which had befallen him on his journey to the home of the gods; and what he said was remembered by those who heard the wonderful stories and told again to their children and their children's children to the latest generations.

Now Gylfe was not the only man who talked with the gods; for Aeger, who lived on the island called Hler's Isle and was also a man of great wisdom, made the journey to Asgard and the gods knew of his coming before he came and prepared a great feast for him. When the feast began Odin had swords brought into the hall and these swords were of such brightness that they lighted the hall without the aid of fire or lamps; and the hall was hung with glittering shields. The gods sat on their thrones and ate and drank with Aeger, and Brage told him strange and wonderful tales of the things which had befallen the gods.

And this is the way in which men came to know the stories which are told in this book.

III. Odin's Search for Wisdom

The wonderful ash-tree, Ygdrasil, made a far-spreading shade against the fierce heat of the sun in summer, and a stronghold against the piercing winds of winter. No man could remember when it had been young. Little children played under its branches, grew to be strong men and women, lived to be old and weary and feeble, and died; and yet the ash-tree gave no signs of decay. Forever preserving its freshness and beauty, it was to live as long as there were men to look upon it, animals to feed under it, birds to flutter among its branches. This mighty ash-tree touched and bound all the worlds together in its wonderful circle of life. One root it sent deep down into the sightless depths of Hel, where the dead lived; another it fastened firmly in Jotunheim, the dreary home of the giants; and with the third it grasped Midgard, the dwelling-place of men. Serpents and all kinds of worms gnawed continually at its roots, but were never able to destroy them. Its branches spread out over the whole earth, and the topmost boughs swayed in the clear air of Asgard itself, rustling against the Valhal, the home of the heroes who had done great deeds or died manfully in battle. At the foot of the tree sat the three Norns, wonderful spinners of fate, who weave the thread of every man's life, making it what they will; and a strange weaving it often was, cut off when the pattern was just beginning to show itself. And every day these Norns sprinkled the tree with the water of life from the Urdar fountain, and so kept it forever green. In the topmost branches sat an eagle singing a strange song about the birth of the world, its decay and death. Under its branches browsed all manner of animals;

among its leaves every kind of bird made its nest; by day the rainbow hung under it; at night the pale northern light flashed over it, and as the winds swept through its rustling branches, the multitudinous murmur of the leaves told strange stories of the past and of the future.

The giants were older than the gods, and knew so much more of the past that the gods had to go to them for wisdom. After a time, however, the gods became wiser than the giants, or they would have ceased to be gods, and been destroyed by the giants, instead of destroying them. When the world was still young, and there were still many things which even the gods had to learn, Odin was so anxious to become wise that he went to a deep well whose waters touched the roots of Ygdrasil itself. The keeper of the well was a very old and very wise giant, named Mimer, or Memory, and he gave no draughts out of the well until he was well paid; for the well contained the water of wisdom, and whoever drank of it became straightway wonderfully wise.

"Give me a draught of this clear water, O Mimer," said Odin, when he had reached the well, and was looking down into its clear, fathomless depths.

Mimer, the keeper, was so old that he could remember everything that had ever happened. His eyes were clear and calm as the stars, his face was noble and restful, and his long white beard flowed down to his waist.

"This water is only to be had at a great price," he said in a wonderfully sweet, majestic tone. "I cannot give to all who ask, but only to those who are able and willing to give greatly in return," he continued.

If Odin had been less of a god he would have thought longer and bargained sharper, but he was so god-like that he cared more to be wise and great than for anything else.

"I will give you whatever you ask," he answered.

Mimer thought a moment. "You must leave an eye," he said at last.

Then he drew up a great draught of the sparkling water, and Odin quenched his divine thirst and went away rejoicing, although he had left an eye behind. Even the gods could not be wise without struggle and toil and sacrifice.

So Odin became the wisest in all the worlds, and there was no god or giant that could contend with him. There was one giant, however, who was called all-wise in Jotunheim, with whom many had contended in knowledge, with curious and difficult questions, and had always been silenced and killed, for then, as now, a man's life often depended on his wisdom. Of this giant, Vafthrudner, and his wisdom many wonderful stories were told, and even among the gods his fame was great. One day as Odin sat thinking of many strange things in the worlds, and many mysterious things in the future, he thought of Vafthrudner. "I will go to Jotunheim and measure wisdom with Vafthrudner, the wisest of the giants," said he to Frigg, his wife, who was sitting by.

Then Frigg remembered those who had gone to contend with the all-wise giant and had never come back, and a fear came over her that the same fate might befall Odin.

"You are wisest in all the worlds, All-Father," she said; "why should you seek a treacherous giant who knows not half so much as you?"

But Odin, who feared nothing, could not be persuaded to stay, and Frigg sadly said good-by as he passed out of Asgard on his journey to Jotunheim. His blue mantle set with stars and his golden helmet he left behind him, and as he journeyed swiftly those who met him saw nothing godlike in him; nor did Vafthrudner when at last he stood at the giant's door.

"I am a simple traveller, Gangraad by name," he said, as Vafthrudner came gruffly toward him. "I ask your hospitality and a chance to strive with you in wisdom." The giant laughed scornfully at the thought of a man coming to contend with him for mastery in knowledge.

"You shall have all you want of both," he growled, "and if you cannot answer my questions you shall never go hence alive."

He did not even ask Odin to sit down, but let him stand in the hall, despising him too much to show him any courtesy. After a time he began to ask questions.

"Tell me, if you can, O wise Gangraad, the name of the river which divides Asgard from Jotunheim."

"The river Ifing, which never freezes over," answered Odin

quickly, as if it were the easiest question in the world; and indeed it was to him, although no man could have answered it. Vafthrudner looked up in great surprise when he heard the reply.

"Good," he said, "you have answered rightly. Tell me, now, the names of the horses that carry day and night across the sky."

Before the words were fairly spoken Odin replied, "Skinfaxe and Hrimfaxe." The giant could not conceal his surprise that a man should know these things.

"Once more," he said quickly, as if he were risking everything on one question; "tell me the name of the plain where the Last Battle will be fought."

This was a terrible question, for the Last Battle was still far off in the future, and only the gods and the greatest of the giants knew where and when it would come. Odin bowed his head when he heard the words, for to be ready for that battle was the divine work of his life, and then said, slowly and solemnly, "On the plain of Vigrid, which is one hundred miles on each side."

Vafthrudner rose trembling from his seat. He knew now that Gangraad was some great one in disguise, and that his own life hung on the answers he himself would soon be forced to make.

"Sit here beside me," he said, "for, whoever you are, worthier antagonist has never entered these walls."

Then they sat down together in the rude stone hall, the mightiest of the gods and the wisest of the giants, and the great contest in wisdom, with a life hanging in either scale, went on between them. Wonderful secrets of the time when no man was and the time when no man will be, those silent walls listened to as Vafthrudner asked Odin one deep question after another, the answer coming swiftly and surely.

After a time the giant could ask no more, for he had exhausted his wisdom.

"It is my turn now," said Odin, and one after another he drew out from Vafthrudner the events of the past, then the wonderful things of the race of giants, and finally he began to question him of that dim, mysterious future whose secrets only the gods know; and as he touched these wonderful things Odin's eyes began to flash, and his form to grow larger and nobler until he seemed no longer the humble Gangraad, but the mighty god he was, and Vafthrudner trembled as he felt the coming doom nearing him with every question.

So hours went by, until at last Odin paused in his swift questioning, stooped down and asked the giant, "What did Odin whisper in the ear of Balder as he ascended the funeral pile?"

Only Odin himself could answer this question, and Vafthrudner replied humbly and with awe, "Who but thyself, All-Father, knoweth the words thou didst say to thy son in the days of old? I have brought my doom upon myself, for in my ignorance I have contended with wisdom itself. Thou art ever the wisest of all."

So Odin conquered, and Wisdom was victorious, as she always has been even when she has contended with giants.

IV. How Odin brought the Mead to Asgard

Besides the gods who lived in Asgard and ruled over Midgard, the world of men, there were the Vans, who ruled the seas and the air. The greatest of these was Njord, who kept the winds in the hollow of his hand and vexed the seas with storms or spread over them the peace of a great calm. His son Frey sent rain and sunshine upon the earth and cared for the harvests, while his daughter Freyja was so full of love that she made the whole world beautiful with tenderness, and filled the hearts of men with the sweetest joys they ever knew.

It happened almost at the beginning that the gods and the Vans went to war with each other, and long and fierce was the struggle between them. When peace was made at last, Njord, Frey, and Freyja found homes for themselves in Asgard, and henceforth they were all as one family.

While the council at which peace was made was being held, a great jar stood in the open space between the two parties, and when the meeting was over the gods were so glad to be rid of the troublesome war that they resolved to create something that should always remind them of the council. So they took the great jar and out of it they moulded the form of a man, and called him Kvaser.

Kvaser was grown up when he was born, and a wonderful man he was too. In all the world there was nobody so wise as he; ask him any question, and he could answer it. He knew how the gods lived, how the world was made, and what sort of places heaven and hell were. Kvaser was good, too, as all really wise men are. He was a great traveller, always going from place to place, and always welcome, because wherever he went he made men wiser and better. People sometimes think poets rather useless sort of men; but that was not the opinion of the gods, for when they made the first poet they made the very best man they could think of.

But poets cannot keep out of trouble any easier than other men, and sometimes not half so well. One night as Kvaser was travelling along through one of those deep valleys that run down to the sea in that country, he came to the house of two dwarfs with very queer names, Galar and Fjalar. They were not only little in size, but small and mean in nature, and like all other people of little nature, they were very envious and cruel, and they hated Kvaser because he was so much nobler than they. Galar had a dark, ugly face, which looked still uglier when he saw Kvaser coming towards the house.

"Fjalar! Fjalar!" he called out, "here comes the wise man who always talks in rhymes, and thinks he knows so much more than anybody else."

And when Fjalar saw the poet walking across the fields, a black shadow came over his face like a thunder-cloud. "Galar," he whispered, looking around to see that nobody could hear, "we've got him alone; let's kill him, and see how much good his wisdom will do him."

Meanwhile Kvaser was slowly approaching the house, and the sea, as it dashed against the rocks, was making a song in his mind. If you had heard him sing it, you would have heard the voices of the waves as they toss their white caps and chase each other foaming and roaring and tumbling on the beach. When Kvaser came up to the dwarfs they pretended to be very glad to see him, and told him he was the one person above all others they had wanted to see, because they had a question they had been waiting a long time to ask him. Kvaser was so noble himself that he never thought evil of any one, and when they asked him to go with them into a very dark and lonely part of the valley, so that nobody could hear their talk, he had no suspicion that they meant any harm; but no sooner had they come to the place than they struck him down from behind. Having killed him, they caught his blood in two jars and a kettle, and mixed it with honey, and so the wonderful mead was made. It took not only sweetness but life to make true poetry.

Not long after this Galar and Fjalar killed a giant named Gilling, and were punished for it too; for the giant's son, Suttung, when he discovered how his father had been put to death, took the dwarfs out to sea and put them on a little rocky island where they would certainly be drowned when the tide came in, and rowed off to leave them; but the rascals begged so hard to be taken off, that he finally promised to let them live if they would give him the mead. Then Suttung took the mead home and put it in his cellar, and told his daughter Gunlad to watch it day and night, for he knew what a precious drink it was. So the mead passed out of the dwarfs' hands into the keeping of a giant.

Now the gods were very fond of Kvaser, and when a long time had passed without any word from him, they asked Galar and Fjalar if they knew anything about him, and the dwarfs said he had been choked by his own wisdom; but Odin knew that this was a false story. He kept his own counsel, and said nothing about what he was going to do, but one day the gods missed him, and knew he had gone on one of his long journeys. As he walked along nobody took him for a god; he looked like a very handsome labourer, and in fact that is what he really was. He had pretty much the whole world in his charge, and he had to work very hard to keep it in any kind of order. Words could hardly describe the beautiful country through which Odin took his way,—its deep, quiet green valleys, with the sparkling cold streams rushing through them; its steep mountains, crowned with fir and pine; its great crags standing out into the sea; and its fjords breaking the coast into numberless bays. Odin enjoyed it all, for the gods love beauty, but he was thinking all the time how he should get the mead out of the giant's cellar. He knew perfectly well that Suttung would never give it up willingly, and that he must get it either by force or by stratagem. Suttung was very strong, and the cellar was cut out of the solid rock; and the more Odin thought about it the harder it seemed to him. If he had been a man he would have given up, but that was not his way; besides, he had loved Kvaser, and the mead was his blood, and he meant to bring it to heaven.

Now Suttung had a brother named Bauge, who was a farmer, and one afternoon, as his nine thralls were mowing in the fields, they saw a stranger coming towards them. It was a very uncommon thing to see a stranger in that out-of-the-way place, and the men all stopped work to watch him. He was a farm labourer like themselves, but he was very large in stature, and had a very noble face and manner.

"A fine meadow of grass," he said in a deep musical voice as he joined them, "but you find it hard work; your scythes are dull."

They certainly did look tired and overworked.

"Hand me your scythes and I will whet them for you," continued the stranger. The thralls were very glad to have anybody do that for them, so they gave him their scythes without saying a word. In a moment the valley rang with the quick strokes of the stone on the hard metal, and the sparks flew in showers around them. The men had never seen such a whetting of scythes before, and their astonishment grew greater still when they found that the grass seemed to fall like magic before them. The mowing, which had been so hard, was now the easiest thing in the world.

"Sell us the whetstone," they shouted, crowding around the stranger.

"Well," said he very coolly, "I will sell it, but I must have a good price for it."

Then each demanded it for himself, and while they were quarrelling as to which should have it, the stranger threw it high into the air, and bade them fight for it, which they did so fiercely that each slew his fellow with his scythe, and the stranger was left alone in the field. He threw the whetstone away, walked off, and as the sun was going down, came to the giant's house and asked if he might stay all night. Bauge was willing, as people were in those days, to give supper and a bed to the stranger, and asked him in.

After supper they talked together, and Bauge told the stranger that his nine thralls had been fighting in the field and had killed each other, and that he was in great trouble because he did not know where to get men to do his work.

"I'll do it," said the stranger.

"Yes," said Bauge, "but you are only one."

"That is true," he answered, "but try me and I'll do the work of all nine."

Bauge looked as if he didn't believe it, but it was one good man gained, at least, and that was something.

"What shall I pay you?" continued Bauge, determined to finish the bargain before the man had time to change his mind. The stranger thought a few moments as if he were uncertain what pay he wanted.

"I'll do the work," he said slowly, at last, "if you will give me a drink of the mead in your brother's cellar." Bauge was very much surprised; he could not understand how the man knew anything about the mead. He was very sure, however, that Suttung would not give him a drop of it, and he thought it was a good chance to get his work done for nothing. "Well," said he, "I can't promise you that, for Suttung takes precious good care of the mead, but I'll do what I can to help you get it."

So the bargain was made, and the next morning the stranger was at work; and all summer, early and late, he was in the fields doing the work of nine men. Bauge often wondered what kind of a man his new farm-hand was; but so long as the work was done he cared for nothing more, and he asked no questions. The stranger once said his name was Bolverk, and that was all he ever said about himself. The months went by, winter came, the work was all done, and Bolverk demanded his pay.

"We'll go and ask my brother about it," said Bauge; so they both went to Suttung. Bauge told his brother the bargain he had made with his workman, and asked for a little of the mead.

"No," said Suttung very crossly, and looking suspiciously at Bolverk; "it's no bargain of mine, and not a drop shall you have."

Bolverk seemed not at all surprised at his ill fortune, and Bauge thought that he had gotten his work done for nothing; but after they had gone a little way together and were hidden from the house by the trees, Bolverk drew out an auger from under his clothing.

"Bauge," said he, "you promised to help me get that mead. I am going into Suttung's cellar for it."

Bauge smiled at the idea of cutting through a thick rock and getting into the cellar with that auger, but when it was handed to him he took it without saying a word and began to bore. It was an astonishing auger, for no sooner had he pressed it against the rock than it began to fly around with wonderful rapidity, the chips of stone fairly making a cloud about him. Once he stopped, for he was afraid he really would get into the cellar, and told Bolverk he had bored through, but Bolverk knew that couldn't be true, because the chips still flew out; so he told Bauge to go on. In a little time the auger slipped through. Bauge looked around, but there was no Bolverk, and while he stared in every direction a large worm crept up the rock and into the hole. When Bauge caught sight of it he thrust the auger hastily into the hole, but Bolverk's voice answered back from the cellar, "Too late, Bauge; you needn't bore any longer."

Then Bauge suspected that a man who had done the work of nine men all summer, and suddenly changed himself into a worm, must be somebody more than common. Bolverk was actually in Suttung's house, but how was he to get out again with the mead?

Gunlad, the young lady who had been charged by her father to watch the precious drink day and night, was sitting quietly beside it, when she was suddenly surprised, and not a little frightened, by the apparition of a young and beautiful man standing before her. What the handsome young man said to her nobody knows, but he probably told her he was very much exhausted, and hinted that she was very lovely; that he had never seen any one he admired so much before. At any rate, he persuaded her to let him drink three draughts of the mead, only three. They were certainly the most astonishing draughts anybody ever heard of, for with the first he emptied one jar, with the second he emptied the other jar, and with the third he finished the kettle.

And now another wonderful change took place. Bolverk had entered as a worm, but no sooner had he drunk the mead than in an instant he became an eagle, and before Gunlad knew what had happened, with splendid wings outspread he was rising upward in broad, easy flight. Through the still air, faster and faster, higher and higher, in wide circles that swept far round the summits of the mountains, in swift majestic flight he rose until the earth had vanished out of sight, and his mighty pinions beat against the gates of Asgard.

So Odin brought the mead to heaven, where it remains to this day, and only those whom the gods love are permitted to drink of it.

V. The Wooing of Gerd

Frey was busy enough in summer, when the sunlight was to fall warm and fruitful along the mountain ridges and deep into the valleys, and the gentle showers were to be gathered far out at sea and driven by the winds across the heavens, weaving soft draperies of mist about the hills, or folding the landscape in with blinding curtains of rain as they passed; for the sowing and the harvesting and the ripening of the fruit were his to watch over and care for. But when winter came, Frey was idle day in and day out, and so it happened, in this long dull season, that he was wandering restlessly one morning about Asgard, when he saw that Odin's throne was empty. To sit upon it and look out over the world was the thought that flashed into Frey's mind and out again, leaving him more idle and restless than before. Neither man nor god, save Odin, had dared to sit in that awful seat, from which nothing was hidden; but when one has nothing to do, it is easy to do wrong. Frey wandered about a little longer, and then boldly mounted the steps and sat down on the throne of the world.

What a wonderful view it was! There lay Asgard beautiful in the morning light; there were the rolling clouds like great waves in the clear heaven; there was the world with its steep mountains and tossing seas; and there was Jotunheim, the home of the giants, gloomy and forbidding,—great black cliffs standing along the coast like grim sentinels. Frey looked long and earnestly at this dreary place where the enemies of the gods lived, hating the sunshine and the summer, and always plotting to bring back winter and barrenness to the earth; and as he looked he saw a massive house standing alone amid the hills. Dark shadows lay across the gloomy landscape, cold winds swept over the sunny valleys, and not one bright or beautiful thing was visible in all the country round. In a moment, however, a figure moved out of the shadows, and a maiden walked slowly to the desolate house, mounted the steps, paused a moment at the door, and then raised her arms to loosen the latch. Straightway a wonderful warmth and light stole over the hills. As she stood with uplifted arms she was so beautiful that earth and air were flooded with her loveliness, and even the heavens were radiant. When she opened the door and closed it behind her the shadows deepened among the hills, and Frey's heart was fast bound among the rocks of Jotunheim. He had been punished for sitting in the seat of Odin.

For days Frey neither ate, slept, nor spoke. He wandered about, silent and gloomy as a cloud, and no one dared ask him why he was so sorrowful. Njord, Frey's father, waited until he could wait no longer, and then with a heavy heart sent for Skirner, whom Frey loved as his own brother, and begged him to find the cause of all this sadness. Skirner came upon Frey walking about with folded arms and eyes cast gloomily upon the ground.

"Why do you stay here all day alone?" he asked. "Where are the light and joy that have always been yours?"

"The sun shines every day, but not for me," answered Frey.

"We were children together," said Skirner, laying his hand on Frey's arm; "we trust each other's truth; tell me your sorrow."

And Frey told him how he had climbed into the seat of Odin and looked upon Jotunheim and seen the beautiful maiden like a sunbeam among shadows, like a sudden coming of summer when snows are deep, and that he could never be happy again until he had won her for himself.

"If that is all, it is easily managed," said Skirner when he had heard the story. "Give me your swiftest horse that can ride through fire and flame, and the sword which swings itself when giants are opposed, and I will go to Jotunheim."

Frey was too glad to get the desire of his heart to delay about giving up the horse and the sword, and Skirner was soon mounted and riding like the wind on his dreary journey. Night came on, the black shadows of the mountains lay across the fjords as he passed, and one by one the endless procession of the stars moved along the summits of the hills as if they would bear him company. All night the hard hoofs rang on the stony way, scattering showers of sparks at every step. Faster and faster the daring rider drove the faithful horse until his flight was like the flash and roar of the thunderbolt.

"Rush on, brave horse," shouted Skirner; "we shall return with the prize or the mighty giant will keep us both."

At last the long journey was over and the gloomy house reached. It was the home of the frost-giant Gymer, and the beautiful maiden who stood at the door when Frey was on Odin's throne was Gerd, the giant's daughter. Fierce dogs were chained about the gate and rushed savagely upon Skirner, barking furiously as if they would tear him limb from limb. So he turned aside and rode up to a shepherd sitting on a mound near by.

"Shepherd, how shall I quiet these dogs and speak with Gymer's daughter?" he asked.

The shepherd looked at him with wonder in his eyes.

"Who are you," he answered, "and whence do you come? Are you doomed to die, or are you a ghost already? Whoever you are, you will never get speech with Gymer's daughter."

"I am not afraid," said Skirner proudly; "fate has already fixed the day of my death, and it cannot be changed."

Skirner's voice rang clear and strong above the howling of the dogs, and Gerd in her chamber heard the brave words.

"What noise is that?" she called to her maidens. "The very earth shakes and the foundations tremble."

One of the maidens looked out and saw Skirner.

"A warrior stands without the wall," she answered; "and while he waits, his horse eats the grass before the gates."

"Bid him enter at once and quaff the pleasant mead, for I fear the slayer of my brother has come."

Skirner needed no second invitation, and, quickly springing to the ground, walked through the stony halls and stood before the beautiful Gerd. She looked keenly at him for a moment and knew from his brightness and beauty that he was from Asgard.

"Are you god, or elf?" she asked; "and why have you come through night and flame to visit Gymer's halls?"

"I am neither elf nor god," said Skirner; "and yet I have come to your home through night and flame. Frey, beautiful among the gods and loved of all the earth, has seen your beauty and can never be happy again until he has won you for himself. I bring you eleven beautiful apples if you will go back with me."

"I will not go," was Gerd's quick answer.

"This wonderful ring, which every ninth night drops eight other rings as rich as itself, shall be yours," said Skirner, holding Draupner in his hand and gently urging her.

Gerd frowned angrily. "I will not take your wondrous ring. I have gold enough in my father's house."

"Then," said Skirner, casting aside his gentleness, "look at this flashing sword! If you will not return I will strike your fair head from your body."

Gerd drew herself up to her full height and answered, with flashing eyes, "I will never be won by force. As for your threats, my father will meet you sword for sword."

"I will quickly slay him," said Skirner angrily. But Gerd only smiled scornfully; she was too cold to be won by gifts and too proud to be moved by threats.

Skirner's face suddenly changed. He drew out a magic wand, and with eyes fixed upon her and in a solemn voice, as he waved it over her, he chanted an awful mystic curse. There was breathless silence in the room while Skirner with slow movements of the wand wove about Gerd dread enchantments and breathed over her the direful incantation:—

"If you refuse, may you sit in everlasting darkness on some dreary mountain top; may terrors crowd round you in awful shapes and tears never cease to fall from your eyes; hated of gods and men, may you pass your life in solitude and desolation!

" 'T is done! I wind the mystic charm;
Thus, thus I trace the giant form;
And three fell characters below,
Fury, and Lust, and Restless Woe.
E'en as I wound, I straight unwind
This fatal spell, if you are kind."[1]

---

1. Andersen's Norse Mythology.

Skirner stopped, and an awful stillness followed. Gerd, trembling under the terrible curse, stood quivering with bowed head and clasped hands. Her pride could not yield, but something told her that to live with a god was better than to stay in the home of a frost-giant. A gentle warmth seemed to steal through and melt her icy coldness. She raised her face, and it was so softened that they hardly knew her.

"I greet you," she said, "with this brimming cup of mead, but I did not think that I should ever love a god."

When Skirner pressed her to go back with him, she promised to meet Frey nine days hence and become his bride in the groves of Bar-isle.

Skirner was soon mounted and riding homeward as fast as his horse could carry him. He was so happy in the thought of Frey's happiness that the distance seemed short, and as he drew near he saw Frey standing before his father's halls, looking anxiously for his coming.

"She is yours!" he shouted, urging his horse into swifter flight.

"When?" said Frey eagerly.

"Nine days hence, in the groves of Bar-isle," joyfully replied Skirner, who expected to be loaded with thanks. Frey, however, was so eager that he forgot what night and flame his friend had ridden through for love of him.

"One day is long; long, indeed, are two. How shall I wait for three?" was all the thanks Skirner got.

The days that followed were long enough for Frey; but even the longest day comes to an end, and at last the ninth day came. Never sun shone so brightly or south wind blew so musically as on the morning when at Bar-isle, under the branches of the great trees, Frey found the beautiful Gerd waiting for his coming, far lovelier than when she stood before her father's door. And the whole earth was happy in them, for while they stood with clasped hands the skies grew soft, the trees put on a tender green, the flowers blossomed along the mountain side, the ripening grain swayed in the fields, and summer lay warm and fragrant over the land.

VI. The Making of the Hammer

One day as Sif, Thor's beautiful wife, was sitting in the palace Bilskirner in Thrudvang, or thunder-world, she fell asleep, with her long hair falling about her shoulders like a shower of gold. She made a very pretty picture as she sat there in the sunlight; at least Loke thought so as he passed by and saw her motionless, like the statue of a goddess in a great temple, instead of a living goddess in her own palace. Loke never saw anything beautiful without the wish that somehow he might spoil it; and when he noticed that Sif was asleep he thought it was a good time to carry off her golden hair, and so rob her of that of which Thor was most proud. As noiselessly as he could, and more like a thief than a god, he stole into the palace, cut off the golden locks and carried them away, without leaving one behind as a trace of his evil deed. When Sif awoke and found her beautiful hair gone, she went and hid herself, lest Thor coming home should miss the beauty which had always been like light to his eyes.

And presently Thor came; but no Sif was there to meet him, making him forget with one proud look from her tender eyes the dangers and labours of his life. She had never failed to greet him at the threshold before; and the strong god's heart, which had never beat a second quicker at sight of the greatest giant in the world, grew faint with fear that in his absence some mishap had befallen her. He ran quickly from room to room in the palace, and at last he came upon Sif, hidden behind a pillar, her shorn head in her hands, weeping bitterly. In a few broken words she told Thor what had happened, and as she went on, Thor's wrath grew hotter and hotter until he was terrible to behold. Lightnings flashed out of his deep-set eyes, the palace trembled under his angry strides, and it seemed as if his fury would burst forth like some awful tempest uprooting and destroying everything in its path.

"I know who did it," he shouted, when Sif had ended her story. "It was that rascally Loke, and I'll break every bone in his thievish body"; and without as much as saying good-by to his sobbing wife, he strode off like a thunder-cloud to Asgard, and there, coming suddenly upon Loke, he seized him by the neck and would have killed him on the spot had not Loke confessed his deed and promised to restore the golden hair.

"I'll get the swarthy elves to make a crown of golden hair for Sif more beautiful than she used to wear," gasped Loke, in the iron grasp of the angry Thor; and Thor, who cared more for Sif's beauty than for Loke's punishment, let the thief go, having bound him by solemn pledges to fulfil his promise without delay.

Loke lost no time, but went far underground to the gloomy smithy of the dwarfs, who were called Ivald's sons, and who were wonderful workers in gold and brass.

"Make me a crown of golden hair," said Loke, "that will grow like any other hair, and I will give you whatever you want for your work."

The bargain was quickly made, and the busy little dwarfs were soon at their task, and in a little time they had done all that Loke asked, and more too; for in addition to the shining hair they gave Loke the spear Gungner and the famous ship Skidbladner.

With these treasures in his arms Loke came into Asgard and began boasting of the wonderful things he had brought from the smithy of Ivald's sons.

"Nobody like the sons of Ivald to work in metal!" he said. "The other dwarfs are all stupid little knaves compared with them."

Now it happened that the dwarf Brok was standing by and heard Loke's boasting; his brother Sindre was so cunning a workman that most of the dwarfs thought him by far the best in the world. It made Brok angry, therefore, to hear the sons of Ivald called the best workmen, and he spoke up and said, "My brother Sindre can make more wonderful things of gold and iron and brass than ever the sons of Ivald thought of."

"Your brother Sindre," repeated Loke scornfully. "Who is your brother Sindre?"

"The best workman in the world," answered Brok.

Loke laughed loud and long. "Go to your wonderful brother Sindre," said he, "and tell him if he can make three such precious things as the spear, the ship, and the golden hair, he shall have my head for his trouble." And Loke laughed longer and louder than before.

Brok was off to the under-world before the laugh died out of his ears, determined to have Loke's head if magic and hard work could do it. He went straight to Sindre and told him of the wager he had laid with Loke, and in a little while Sindre was hard at work in his smithy. It was a queer place for such wonderful work as was done in it, for it was nothing but a great cavern underground, with tools piled up in little heaps around its sides, and thick darkness everywhere when the furnace fire was not sending its glow out into the blackness. If you had looked in now, you would have seen a broad glare of light streaming out from the furnace, for Brok was blowing the bellows with all his might, and the coals were fairly blazing with heat. When all was ready Sindre took a swine-skin, put it into the furnace, and telling Brok to blow the bellows until his return, went out of the smithy. Brok kept steadily at work, although a gad-fly flew in, buzzed noisily about, and, finally settling on his hand, stung him so that he could hardly bear it. After a while Sindre came back and took out of the furnace a wonderful boar with bristles of pure gold.

Then Sindre took some gold, and placing it in the furnace bade Brok blow as if his life depended on it, and went out a second time. Brok had no sooner begun blowing than the troublesome gad-fly came back, and fastening upon his neck stung him so fiercely that he could hardly keep his hands away from his neck; but Brok was a faithful dwarf, who meant to do his work thoroughly if he died for it, and so he blew away as if it were the easiest thing in the world, until Sindre came back and took a shining ring from the fire. The third time Sindre put iron into the fire, and bidding Brok blow without ceasing, went out again. No sooner had he gone than the gad-fly flew in, and settling between Brok's eyes stung him so sharply that drops of blood ran down into his eyes, and he could not see what he was doing. He blew away as bravely as he could for some time, but the pain was so keen, and he was so blind, that at last he raised his hand quickly to brush the fly away. That very instant Sindre returned.

"You have almost spoiled it," he said, as he took out of the glowing furnace the wonderful hammer Mjolner. "See how short you have made the handle! But you can't lengthen it now. So carry the gifts to Asgard, and bring me Loke's head."

Brok started off with the golden boar, the shining ring, and the terrible hammer.

When he came through the great gate of Asgard the gods were very anxious to see the end of this strange contest, and taking their seats on their shining thrones they appointed Odin, Thor, and Frey to judge between Loke and Brok, as to which had the most wonderful things. Then Loke brought out the spear Gungner, which never misses its mark, and gave it to Odin; and the golden hair he gave to Thor, who placed it on Sif's head, and straightway it began to grow like any other hair, and Sif was as beautiful as on the day when Loke saw her in Thor's palace, and robbed her of her tresses; and to Frey he gave the marvellous ship Skidbladner, which always found a breeze to drive it wherever its master would go, no matter how the sea was running, nor from what quarter the wind was blowing, and which could be folded up and carried in one's pocket. Then Loke laughed scornfully.

"Bring out the trinkets which that wonderful brother of yours has made," he said.

Brok came forward, and stood before the wondering gods with his treasures.

"This ring," said he, handing it to Odin, "will cast off, every ninth night, eight other rings as pure and heavy as itself. This boar," giving it to Frey, "will run more swiftly in the air, and on the sea, by night or by day, than the swiftest horse, and no night will be so dark, no world so gloomy, that the shining of these bristles shall not make it light as noonday. And this hammer," placing Mjolner in Thor's strong hands, "shall never fail, no matter how big nor how hard that which it smites may be; no matter how far it is thrown, it will always return to your hand; you may make it so small that it can be hidden in your bosom, and its only fault is the shortness of its handle."

Thor swung it round his head, and lightning flashed and flamed through Asgard, deep peals of thunder rolled through the sky, and mighty masses of cloud piled quickly up about him. The gods gathered around, and passed the hammer from one to the other, saying that it would be their greatest protection against their enemies, the frost-giants, who were always trying to force their way into Asgard, and they declared that Brok had won the wager. Brok's swarthy little face was as bright as his brother's furnace fire, so delighted was he to have beaten the boastful Loke. But how was he to get his wager, now he had won it? It was no easy matter to take the head off a god's shoulders. Brok thought a moment. "I will take Loke's head," he said finally, thinking some of the other gods might help him.

"I will give you whatever you want in place of my head," growled Loke, angry that he was beaten, and having no idea of paying his wager by losing his head.

"I will have your head or I will have nothing," answered the plucky little dwarf, determined not to be cheated out of his victory.

"Well, then, take it," shouted Loke; but by the time Brok reached the place where he had been standing, Loke was far away, for he wore shoes with which he could run through the air or over the water. Then Brok asked Thor to find Loke and bring him back, which Thor did promptly, for the gods always saw to it that people kept their promises. When Loke was brought back Brok wanted to cut his head off at once.

"You may cut off my head, but you have no right to touch my neck," said Loke, who was cunning, as well as wicked. That was true, and of course the head could not be taken off without touching the neck, so Brok had to give it up.

But he determined to do something to make Loke feel that he had won his wager, so he took an awl and a thong and sewed his lips together so tightly that he could make no more boastings.

VII. Odin in Geirrod's Palace

It was as lovely a morning as ever dawned when Geirrod and Agnar, sons of old King Hraudung, pushed their boat out from the rocky shore for a day's fishing. The sky overhead was as blue as Odin's wonderful mantle; and the sea beneath them as blue as the sky. They could see the mountain tops far off behind them and every rock along the beach for miles and miles away. It was happiness just to be out of doors in such weather, and as the rowers bent to their work there was such strength and joy in them that the boat skimmed over the water like a living thing. When they were fairly out where the wind blew freshly and the waves danced merrily, they let their lines into the sea and began to lay wagers on the luck. Geirrod, who was selfish and pushing, generally got the best of things, and was very certain that he would carry home more fish than Agnar. But before they had talked much about it they were too busy to talk at all. Such luck befell them as they had never had before. No sooner did the line touch the water than it was travelling off in the mouth of some hungry fish who was quickly landed in the bottom of the boat. All the morning the boys were so busy that they did not once look at the sky, and when the sun began to sink a little toward the west they took no thought of the dark clouds scudding along overhead nor of the rising wind whistling over the white caps. And while they let down and drew up their lines the sky grew darker and darker, until not a spot of blue was to be seen anywhere, and the wind rose higher and higher, driving the sea in spray before it.

When at last the storm broke on Geirrod and Agnar it was too late to reach the shore. The waves ran so high that the boat was almost swamped in the trough of the sea, and the next minute the angry waters had snatched both oars out of the hands of the rowers and flung them far off to leeward. There was nothing to do but to sit still and be carried on by wave and wind. The boys were good Norsemen, and though they were drenched to the skin, and blinded by spray, they were cool and brave. The roar of the sea and the tempest was sweeter music in their ears than the melody of harp-strings in their father's palace. Holding on as best they could they watched the rushing clouds until darkness fell on the sea and they were alone with the tempest. They could not speak to each other, for the uproar of the wind and the waves drowned all other sounds; they could do nothing; they could only wait; and as they waited the night wore on. Suddenly there came a sound they both knew, and which made even their bold hearts beat a little faster,—the sound of the breakers. They strained their eyes, peering anxiously into the darkness, but not a thing could they see. They were driven on faster and faster, until a mighty wave lifted the boat a moment in mid-air and then flung it broken and shattered on to the rocks.

How Geirrod and Agnar got ashore they could never tell. They remembered nothing but an awful crash, a blinding rush of waters, and then, coming slowly back to life they found themselves bruised and bleeding on the shore of an island far off the coast they had sailed from. When morning broke at last, clear and cold, as if the earth had been made over instead of torn to pieces in the night, they made their way slowly and painfully back from the shore. They had gone but a little way when they were overjoyed to see a thin column of smoke rising into the clear air, and a moment after they were at the door of a little farm-house. The farmer was very poor, for the island was small and rocky, but he had a striking form, and a face more noble than any the boys had ever seen at their father's court.

"We have been wrecked upon this island," said Geirrod, who was always the first to speak. "Can you give us food?"

The farmer looked at them thoughtfully, as if he saw a great deal in their faces that was interesting.

"Certainly we can," said he, in a deep, musical voice. "No man ever went hungry from Grimner's door. Here, wife," turning back to the open door, "set what you have before these young sailors."

Geirrod and Agnar had sat at kings' tables all their lives, but they had never eaten at such a feast as the farmer's good wife spread for them on the plain table. Like her husband, she was very large of form and beautiful of feature, and she looked as if she might be the mother of half of the world, as indeed she was, and of the other half too. Breakfast over, the boys told the story of their parentage, their fishing, the storm and the wreck, the farmer glancing at his wife, from time to time, as if it greatly pleased him.

"Boys," said he when the story was told, "the season changed with the storm which brought you here. Winter has set in, and you must stay under our roof until spring. The house is not very large, but it will keep us all, I trust."

The good wife nodded approval, and the boys themselves were not sorry to stay, so great a fancy had they already taken to the pair. What a winter that was! The days were so short that they could hardly be called days at all. The cold was bitter, the winds roared about the little island, and the sea rushed upon it as if it meant to sweep the little piece of earth out of sight forever; but the boys cared for none of these things. Agnar spent all his time with the farmer's wife, and learned to love her as if she were his mother; but Geirrod never left Grimner's side for an hour if he could help it. Never was there such a farmer before. He seemed to know everything, and he was willing to tell the boy all he knew himself. He told him stories of the strong and valiant Norsemen who had made perilous voyages and performed mighty deeds of valour; he described the wonders of the heavens and the secrets of the sea and the mysteries of earth; he even once or twice spoke of the gods themselves, and of Asgard, where they dwelt a glorious company of strong spirits; and when he spoke of these things his eyes flashed and his form grew so large that he seemed to Geirrod no longer the island farmer, but a god in human guise. He spoke of courage too, and of honour, truthfulness and hospitality, until the boy's selfish heart grew generous for a little while, and he wanted to do some noble thing himself.

In such talks as these, and with short wanderings about the storm-beaten shores of the island, the winter passed quickly away, and before the boys were ready to go the sky had grown soft and the water calm again. Grimner built a new boat for them, and one morning, when all was ready, they pushed out, with many farewells, from the home that had sheltered them so many months, and rowed swiftly homeward. Grimner's last earnest word to Geirrod was, "Be true and noble." But Geirrod was too selfish to carry away the great thoughts which the farmer had given him; the burning words, the stories of great deeds he had listened to had made him ambitious to be strong, but not to be good. No sooner were the boys afloat than evil thoughts took possession of him and held him until the boat touched shore on the mainland, and then they mastered him entirely, so that he sprang out on to the land and gave the boat a mighty lurch back into the sea, shouting to Agnar, "Go away and may the evil spirits seize you!"

Then, without looking back, he hastened to the palace, where he was at once greeted as King, for his father was dead. Agnar, after many adventures, landed in a far-off part of the country, and ended by marrying a giantess.

Years passed away, and Geirrod had almost forgotten the evil he had done his brother; but the Fates never let the sins of men go unpunished. It happened one day that as Odin, the father of the gods and of men, and his wife Frigg were sitting upon their throne overlooking the whole earth, they spoke of the boys who had been with them on the island; for the farmer Grimner and his wife were none other than the greatest of the gods.

"Look at Agnar," said Odin, "whom you brought up, wasting his time with a giantess, while my foster son Geirrod rules his kingdom right royally."

Now although Frigg was a goddess, she had some weaknesses like the rest of us, and she was annoyed that her teaching had done so little for Agnar, and that Odin should notice it too, so she answered, "It's all very well to talk about Geirrod's reigning right royally, but he is no true King, for he puts his guests to torture."

Odin was indignant that such a charge should be brought against his favourite, and after much dispute the two laid a wager, and Odin said he would visit Geirrod in disguise and settle the matter himself.

Now Geirrod was not really inhospitable, but Frigg sent word to him to keep a sharp look-out for a dangerous wizard who was coming his way; and so it happened that one morning when a very old man, in a long robe of grey fur, stopped at the door and asked shelter, the King had him brought into the great council chamber, and began to question him. He asked him who he was, from what country he came, and what was the end of his journey, but not a word would the old man answer. Whereupon Geirrod, getting very angry and not a little frightened, had two fires built on the stone floor, and bound the stranger between them. Eight days the old man sat there in the awful heat, silent and motionless. No one gave him a thought of pity or a word of comfort save little Agnar, Geirrod's son, who brought him a cooling drink, and told him how cruel he thought his father was. On the last day the fires had crept so near that the fur coat began to burn, and then suddenly the old man found his voice, and what a voice it was! It filled the council chamber like the tones of some great organ, so sweet and deep and wonderful it was. Bound between the blazing flames that joined their fiery tongues above his head and beat fiercely against the vaulted roof, the old man broke into such a song as had never been heard on earth before. He sang the birth of gods, the glories of Asgard, the secrets of fate, such things as only Odin himself could know; and as the song deepened in its tone, and the awful secrets of the other world were revealed, Geirrod's throne trembled beneath him, for in the tortured stranger he saw now the mighty Odin himself. He started up to break the bonds and scatter the flaming brands, dropped his sword, caught it by a swift thrust, slipped suddenly, fell on the glittering blade, and rolled dead at Odin's feet. His sin was punished. Odin vanished, and little Agnar was King.

VIII. The Apples of Idun

Once upon a time Odin, Loke, and Hoener started on a journey. They had often travelled together before on all sorts of errands, for they had a great many things to look after, and more than once they had fallen into trouble through the prying, meddlesome, malicious spirit of Loke, who was never so happy as when he was doing wrong. When the gods went on a journey they travelled fast and hard, for they were strong, active spirits who loved nothing so much as hard work, hard blows, storm, peril, and struggle. There were no roads through the country over which they made their way, only high mountains to be climbed by rocky paths, deep valleys into which the sun hardly looked during half the year, and swift-rushing streams, cold as ice, and treacherous to the surest foot and the strongest arm. Not a bird flew through the air, not an animal sprang through the trees. It was as still as a desert. The gods walked on and on, getting more tired and hungry at every step. The sun was sinking low over the steep, pine-crested mountains, and the travellers had neither breakfasted nor dined. Even Odin was beginning to feel the pangs of hunger, like the most ordinary mortal, when suddenly, entering a little valley, the famished gods came upon a herd of cattle. It was the work of a minute to kill a great ox and to have the carcass swinging in a huge pot over a roaring fire.

But never were gods so unlucky before! In spite of their hunger the pot would not boil. They piled on the wood until the great flames crackled and licked the pot with their fiery tongues, but every time the cover was lifted there was the meat just as raw as when it was put in. It is easy to imagine that the travellers were not in very good humor. As they were talking about it, and wondering how it could be, a voice called out from the branches of the oak overhead, "If you will give me my fill I'll make the pot boil."

The gods looked first at each other and then into the tree, and there they discovered a great eagle. They were glad enough to get their supper on almost any terms, so they told the eagle he might have what he wanted if he would only get the meat cooked. The bird was as good as his word, and in less time than it takes to tell it supper was ready. Then the eagle flew down and picked out both shoulders and both legs. This was a pretty large share, it must be confessed, and Loke, who was always angry when anybody got more than he, no sooner saw what the eagle had taken than he seized a great pole and began to beat the rapacious bird unmercifully. Whereupon a very singular thing happened, as singular things always used to happen when the gods were concerned: the pole struck fast in the huge talons of the eagle at one end, and Loke stuck fast at the other end. Struggle as he might, he could not get loose, and as the great bird sailed away over the tops of the trees, Loke went pounding along on the ground, striking against rocks and branches until he was bruised half to death.

The eagle was not an ordinary bird by any means, as Loke soon found when he begged for mercy. The giant Thjasse happened to be flying abroad in his eagle plumage when the hungry travellers came under the oak and tried to cook the ox. It was into his hands that Loke had fallen, and he was not to get away until he had promised to pay roundly for his freedom.

If there was one thing which the gods prized above their other treasures in Asgard, it was the beautiful fruit of Idun, kept by the goddess in a golden casket and given to the gods to keep them forever young and fair. Without these Apples all their power could not have kept them from getting old like the meanest of mortals. Without these Apples of Idun Asgard itself would have lost its charm; for what would heaven be without youth and beauty forever shining through it?

Thjasse told Loke that he could not go unless he would promise to bring him the Apples of Idun. Loke was wicked enough for anything; but when it came to robbing the gods of their immortality, even he hesitated. And while he hesitated the eagle dashed hither and thither, flinging him against the sides of the mountains and dragging him through the great tough boughs of the oaks until his courage gave out entirely, and he promised to steal the Apples out of Asgard and give them to the giant.

Loke was bruised and sore enough when he got on his feet again to hate the giant who handled him so roughly, with all his heart, but he was not unwilling to keep his promise to steal the Apples, if only for the sake of tormenting the other gods. But how was it to be done? Idun guarded the golden fruit of immortality with sleepless watchfulness. No one ever touched it but herself, and a beautiful sight it was to see her fair hands spread it forth for the morning feasts in Asgard. The power which Loke possessed lay not so much in his own strength, although he had a smooth way of deceiving people, as in the goodness of others who had no thought of his doing wrong because they never did wrong themselves.

Not long after all this happened, Loke came carelessly up to Idun as she was gathering her Apples to put them away in the beautiful carven box which held them.

"Good morning, goddess," said he. "How fair and golden your Apples are!"

"Yes," answered Idun; "the bloom of youth keeps them always beautiful."

"I never saw anything like them," continued Loke slowly, as if he were talking about a matter of no importance, "until the other day."

Idun looked up at once with the greatest interest and curiosity in her face. She was very proud of her Apples, and she knew no earthly trees, however large and fair, bore the immortal fruit.

"Where have you seen any Apples like them?" she asked.

"Oh, just outside the gates," said Loke indifferently. "If you care to see them I'll take you there. It will keep you but a moment. The tree is only a little way off."

Idun was anxious to go at once.

"Better take your Apples with you to compare them with the others," said the wily god, as she prepared to go.

Idun gathered up the golden Apples and went out of Asgard, carrying with her all that made it heaven. No sooner was she beyond the gates than a mighty rushing sound was heard, like the coming of a tempest, and before she could think or act, the giant Thjasse, in his eagle plumage, was bearing her swiftly away through the air to his desolate, icy home in Thrymheim, where, after vainly trying to persuade her to let him eat the Apples and be forever young like the gods, he kept her a lonely prisoner.

Loke, after keeping his promise and delivering Idun into the hands of the giant, strayed back into Asgard as if nothing had happened. The next morning, when the gods assembled for their feast, there was no Idun. Day after day went past, and still the beautiful goddess did not come. Little by little the light of youth and beauty faded from the home of the gods, and they themselves became old and haggard. Their strong, young faces were lined with care and furrowed by age, their raven locks passed from gray to white, and their flashing eyes became dim and hollow. Brage, the god of poetry, could make no music while his beautiful wife was gone he knew not whither.

Morning after morning the faded light broke on paler and ever paler faces, until even in heaven the eternal light of youth seemed to be going out forever.

Finally the gods could bear the loss of power and joy no longer. They made rigorous inquiry. They tracked Loke on that fair morning when he led Idun beyond the gates; they seized him and brought him into solemn council, and when he read in their haggard faces the deadly hate which flamed in all their hearts against his treachery, his courage failed, and he promised to bring Idun back to Asgard if the goddess Freyja would lend him her falcon-guise. No sooner said than done; and with eager gaze the gods watched him as he flew away, becoming at last only a dark moving speck against the sky.

After long and weary flight Loke came to Thrymheim, and was glad enough to find Thjasse gone to sea and Idun alone in his dreary house. He changed her instantly into a nut, and taking her thus disguised in his talons, flew away as fast as his falcon wings could carry him. And he had need of all his speed, for Thjasse, coming suddenly home and finding Idun and her precious fruit gone, guessed what had happened, and, putting on his eagle plumage, flew forth in a mighty rage, with vengeance in his heart. Like the rushing wings of a tempest, his mighty pinions beat the air and bore him swiftly onward. From mountain peak to mountain peak he measured his wide course, almost grazing at times the murmuring pine forests, and then sweeping high in mid-air with nothing above but the arching sky, and nothing beneath but the tossing sea.

At last he sees the falcon far ahead, and now his flight becomes like the flash of the lightning for swiftness, and like the rushing of clouds for uproar. The haggard faces of the gods line the walls of Asgard and watch the race with tremulous eagerness. Youth and immortality are staked upon the winning of Loke. He is weary enough and frightened enough too, as the eagle sweeps on close behind him; but he makes desperate efforts to widen the distance between them. Little by little the eagle gains on the falcon. The gods grow white with fear; they rush off and prepare great fires upon the walls. With fainting, drooping wing the falcon passes over and drops exhausted by the wall. In an instant the fires have been lighted, and the great flames roar to heaven. The eagle sweeps across the fiery line a second later, and falls, maimed and burned, to the ground, where a dozen fierce hands smite the life out of him, and the great giant Thjasse perishes among his foes.

Idun resumes her natural form as Brage rushes to meet her. The gods crowd round her. She spreads the feast, the golden Apples gleaming with unspeakable lustre in the eyes of the gods. They eat; and once more their faces glow with the beauty of immortal youth, their eyes flash with the radiance of divine power, and, while Idun stands like a star for beauty among the throng, the song of Brage is heard once more; for poetry and immortality are wedded again.

IX. Thor goes a Fishing

Midway between Niflheim and Muspelheim lay Midgard, the home of men, its round disk everywhere encircled by the ocean, which perpetually rushed upon it, gently in still summer afternoons, but with a terrible uproar in winter. Ages ago, when the Midgard-serpent had grown so vast that even the gods were afraid of him, Odin cast him into the sea, and he lay flat at the bottom of the ocean, grown to such monstrous size that his scaly length encircled the whole world. Holding the end of his tail in his mouth, he sometimes lay motionless for weeks at a time, and looking across the water no one would have dreamed that such a monster was asleep in its depths. But when the Midgard-serpent was aroused his wrath was terrible to behold. He lashed the ocean into great sheets of foam, he piled the waves mountain high, he dashed the spray into the very heavens, and woe to the galleys that were sailing homeward.

It happened once that the gods were feasting with Aeger, the sea-god, and the ale gave out, and Aeger had no kettle in which to brew a new supply.

"Thor," said Aeger, after he had thought a moment, "will you get me a kettle?"

Thor was always ready for any hard or dangerous thing.

"Of course I will," was his quick reply, "only tell me where to get one."

That, however, was no easy thing to do. Kettles big enough to brew ale for Asgard were not to be picked up at a moment's notice. Everybody wanted more ale, but nobody could tell Thor where to find a kettle, until Tyr, the god of courage, spoke up:

"East of the rivers Elivagar lives my father, Hymer, who has a kettle marvellously strong and one mile deep."

This was large enough even for the gods.

"Do you think we can get it?" asked Thor, who always wanted to succeed in his undertakings.

"If we cannot get it by force we can by stratagem," answered Tyr, and they started off at once, Thor taking the disguise of a young man. The goats drew them swiftly to Egil, with whom Thor left them while he and Tyr pushed on to finish the journey afoot. It was rough and perilous travelling, but they reached Hymer's hall without accident, and there Tyr found his grandmother, a frightfully ugly giantess, and his mother, a wonderfully beautiful woman, with fair hair, and a face so radiant that the sun seemed to be always shining upon it. The latter advised them to hide under the great kettles in the hall, because when Hymer came home in bad temper he was sometimes cruel to strangers.

Late in the evening Hymer came home from his fishing. A cold wind swept through the hall as he entered, his eyes were piercing as the stars on a winter's night, and his beard was white with frost.

"I welcome you home," said Tyr's beautiful mother; "our son, for whom we have been looking so long, has come home, bringing with him the enemy of giants and the protector of Asgard. See how they hide themselves behind that pillar yonder."

She pointed to a pillar at the farther end of the hall. Hymer turned and looked at it with his piercing, icy glance, and in an instant it snapped into a thousand pieces; the beam overhead broke, and eight kettles fell with a crash on the stone floor. Only one out of the eight remained unbroken, and from it Thor and Tyr came forth. Hymer was not glad to see Thor standing there under his own roof, but he could not turn him out, so he made the best of it and ordered three oxen to be served for supper. Thor had travelled a long distance and was very hungry, and ate two of the oxen before he was satisfied.

"If you eat like that," said Hymer, "we will have to live on fish to-morrow."

Early the next morning, before the sun was up, Thor heard

Hymer getting ready for a day of fishing. He dressed himself quickly and went out to the giant. "Good morning, Hymer," he said pleasantly. "I am fond of fishing; let me row out to sea with you."

"Oho," answered the giant scornfully, not at all pleased with the idea of having his powerful enemy in the boat with him, "such a puny young fellow can be of no use to me, and if I go as far out to sea as I generally do, and stay as long, you will catch a cold that will be the death of you."

Thor was so angry at this insult that he wanted to let his hammer ring on the giant's head, but he wisely kept his temper.

"I will row as far from the land as you care to go," was his answer, "and it is by no means certain that I shall be the first to want to put in again. What do you bait with?"

"Find a bait for yourself," was the giant's surly reply.

Thor ran up to a herd of Hymer's cattle, seized the largest bull, wrung off its head without any trouble, and put it in the boat. Then they both pushed off and were soon rowing seaward. Thor rowed aft, and the boat fairly shot through the water. Hymer could pull a strong oar, but he had never seen such a stroke as Thor's before. The boat fairly trembled under the force of it. In a few moments they reached Hymer's fishing-ground, and he called out to Thor to stop.

"Oh, no, not yet," said Thor, bending steadily over his oars; "we must go a good distance beyond this."

Thor pulled with such tremendous power that they were soon far out to sea, and Hymer began to be frightened.

"If you don't stop," he called out, "we shall be over the Midgard-serpent."

Thor paid no attention, but rowed on until they were far out of sight of land and about where he thought the great snake was coiled in the bottom of the sea; then he laid down the oars as fresh and strong apparently as when he got into the boat. It was the strangest fishing party the world ever saw, and the most wonderful fishing. No sooner had Hymer's bait touched water than it was seized by two whales. Thor smiled quietly at the giant's luck, took out a fishing-line, made with wonderful skill, and so strong that it could not be broken, fastened the bull's head upon the hook and cast it into the sea. The Midgard-serpent instantly seized it, and in a second the hook was fast in its palate. Then came a furious struggle between the strong god and the terrible monster which was the dread of the whole earth.

Stung by the pain, the serpent writhed and pulled so hard that Thor had to brace himself against the side of the boat. When he found that the snake had taken his hook his wrath rose, and his divine strength came upon him. He pulled the line with such tremendous force that his feet went straight through the bottom of the boat, and he stood on the bed of the ocean while he drew the snake up to the side of the boat. The monster, convulsed with pain, reared its terrible head out of the water, its glittering eyes flashing, its whole vast body writhing and churning the ocean into a whirlpool of eddying foam. Thor's eyes blazed with wrath, and he held the serpent in a grasp like a vise. The uproar was like a terrible storm, and the boat, the fishers, and the snake were hidden by columns of foam that rose in the air. No one can tell what the end would have been if Hymer, trembling with fright and seeing the boat about to sink, had not sprung forward and cut the line just as Thor was raising his hammer to crush the serpent's head. The snake sank at once to the bottom of the sea, and Thor, turning upon the giant, struck him such a blow under the ear that he fell headlong into the water. The giant got back to the boat, however, and they rowed to land, taking the two whales with them.

When they reached shore Thor was still filled with rage at the meddlesome giant, because he had lost him the serpent, but he quietly picked up the boat and carried it home, Hymer taking the whales. Once more under his own roof, the giant's courage returned, and he challenged Thor to show his strength by breaking his drinking-cup. Thor sat down and, taking the cup, hurled it against a pillar. It flew through the air, crashed against the stone, bounded back, and was picked up as whole and perfect as when it came into Thor's hands. He was puzzled, but Tyr's beautiful fair-haired mother whispered to him, "Throw it at Hymer's forehead; it is harder than any drinking-cup."

Thor drew in all his god-like strength and dashed the cup with a terrific effort at Hymer. The forehead was unharmed, but the cup was scattered in a thousand pieces over the floor. Hymer had lost a great treasure by the experiment, but he only said, "That drink was too hot. Perhaps you will take the kettle off now," he added with a sneer.

Tyr immediately laid hands on the kettle, but he could not move it an inch. Then Thor took the great pot in his hands and drew it up with such a mighty effort that his feet went through the stone floor of the hall, but he lifted it and, placing it on his head like a mighty helmet, walked off, the rings of the kettle clanging about his feet. The two gods walked swiftly away from the hall where so many troubles and labours had awaited them, and it was a long time before Thor turned to look back. When he did, it was not a moment too soon, for Hymer was close behind, with a multitude of many-headed giants, in hot pursuit.

In one minute Thor had lifted the kettle off his head and put it on the ground, in another he was swinging the hammer among the giants, and in another, when the lightnings had gone out and the thunder had died in awful echoes among the hills, Tyr and Thor were alone on the field.

They went on to Egil, mounted the chariot and drove the goats swiftly on to Aeger's, where the gods were impatiently waiting for the kettle. There was straightway a mighty brewing of ale, Thor told the story of his adventures in search of the kettle, and the feast went merrily on.

X. How Thor found his Hammer

The frost-giants were always trying to get into Asgard. For more than half the year they held the world in their grasp, locking up the streams in their rocky beds, hushing their music and the music of the birds as well, and leaving nothing but a wild waste of desolation under the cold sky. They hated the warm sunshine which stirred the wild flowers out of their sleep, and clothed the steep mountains with verdure, and set all the birds a-singing in the swaying tree-tops. They hated the beautiful god Balder, with whose presence summer came back to the ice-bound earth, and, above all, they hated Thor, whose flashing hammer drove them back into Jotunheim, and guarded the summer sky with its sudden gleamings of power. So long as Thor had his hammer Asgard was safe against the giants.

One morning Thor started up out of a long, deep sleep, and put out his hand for the hammer; but no hammer was there. Not a sign of it could be found anywhere, although Thor anxiously searched for it. Then a thought of the giants came suddenly in his mind; and his anger rose till his eyes flashed like great fires, and his red beard trembled with wrath.

"Look, now, Loke," he shouted, "they have stolen Mjolner by enchantment, and no one on earth or in heaven knows where they have hidden it."

"We will get Freyja's falcon-guise and search for it," answered Loke, who was always quick to get into trouble or to get out of it again. So they went quickly to Folkvang and found Freyja surrounded by her maidens and weeping tears of pure gold, as she had always done since her husband went on his long journey.

"The hammer has been stolen by enchantment," said Thor. "Will you lend me the falcon-guise that I may search for it?"

"If it were silver, or even gold, you should have it and welcome," answered Freyja, glad to help Thor find the wonderful hammer that kept them all safe from the hands of the frost-giants.

So the falcon-guise was brought, and Loke put it on and flew swiftly out of Asgard to the home of the giants. His great wings made broad shadows over the ripe fields as he swept along, and the reapers, looking up from their work, wondered what mighty bird was flying seaward. At last he reached Jotunheim, and no sooner had he touched ground and taken off the falcon-guise than he came upon the giant Thrym, sitting on a hill twisting golden collars for his dogs and stroking the long manes of his horses.

"Welcome, Loke," said the giant. "How fares it with the gods and the elves, and what has brought you to Jotunheim?"

"It fares ill with both gods and elves since you stole Thor's hammer," replied Loke, guessing quickly that Thrym was the thief; "and I have come to find where you have hidden it."

Thrym laughed as only a giant can when he knows he has made trouble for somebody.

"You won't find it," he said at last. "I have buried it eight miles under ground, and no one shall take it away unless he gets Freyja for me as my wife."

The giant looked as if he meant what he said, and Loke, seeing no other way of finding the hammer, put on his falcon-guise and flew back to Asgard. Thor was waiting to hear what news he brought, and both were soon at the great doors of Folkvang.

"Put on your bridal dress, Freyja," said Thor bluntly, after his fashion, "and we will ride swiftly to Jotunheim."

But Freyja had no idea of marrying a giant just to please Thor; and, in fact, that Thor should ask her to do such a thing threw her into such a rage that the floor shook under her angry tread, and her necklace snapped in pieces.

"Do you think I am a weak lovesick girl, to follow you to Jotunheim and marry Thrym?" she cried indignantly.

Finding they could do nothing with Freyja, Thor and Loke

called all the gods together to talk over the matter and decide what should be done to get back the hammer. The gods were very much alarmed, because they knew the frost-giants would come upon Asgard as soon as they knew the hammer was gone. They said little, for they did not waste time with idle words, but they thought long and earnestly, and still they could find no way of getting hold of Mjolner once more. At last Heimdal, who had once been a Van, and could therefore look into the future, said: "We must have the hammer at once or Asgard will be in danger. If Freyja will not go, let Thor be dressed up and go in her place. Let keys jingle from his waist and a woman's dress fall about his feet. Put precious stones upon his breast, braid his hair like a woman's, hang the necklace around his neck, and bind the bridal veil around his head."

Thor frowned angrily. "If I dress like a woman," he said, "you will jeer at me."

"Don't talk of jeers," retorted Loke; "unless that hammer is brought back quickly the giants will rule in our places."

Thor said no more, but allowed himself to be dressed like a bride, and soon drove off to Jotunheim with Loke beside him disguised as a servant-maid. There was never such a wedding journey before. They rode in Thor's chariot and the goats drew them, plunging swiftly along the way, thunder pealing through the mountains and the frightened earth blazing and smoking as they passed. When Thrym saw the bridal party coming he was filled with delight.

"Stand up, you giants," he shouted to his companions; "spread cushions upon the benches and bring in Freyja, my bride. My yards are full of golden-horned cows, black oxen please my gaze whichever way I look, great wealth and many treasures are mine, and Freyja is all I lack."

It was evening when the bride came driving into the giant's court in her blazing chariot. The feast was already spread against her coming, and with her veil modestly covering her face she was seated at the great table, Thrym fairly beside himself with delight. It wasn't every giant who could marry a goddess!

If the bridal journey had been so strange that any one but a foolish giant would have hesitated to marry a wife who came in such a turmoil of fire and storm, her conduct at the table ought certainly to have put Thrym on his guard; for never had bride such an appetite before. The great tables groaned under the load of good things, but they were quickly relieved of their burden by the voracious bride. She ate a whole ox before the astonished giant had fairly begun to enjoy his meal. Then she devoured eight large salmon, one after the other, without stopping to take breath; and having eaten up the part of the feast specially prepared for the hungry men, she turned upon the delicacies which had been made for the women, and especially for her own fastidious appetite.

Thrym looked on with wondering eyes, and at last, when she had added to these solid foods three whole barrels of mead, his amazement was so great that, his astonishment getting the better of his politeness, he called out, "Did any one ever see such an appetite in a bride before, or know a maid who could drink so much mead?"

Then Loke, who was playing the part of a serving-maid, thinking that the giant might have some suspicions, whispered to him, "Freyja was so happy in the thought of coming here that she has eaten nothing for eight whole days."

Thrym was so pleased at this evidence of affection that he leaned forward and raised the veil as gently as a giant could, but he instantly dropped it and sprang back the whole length of the hall before the bride's terrible eyes.

"Why are Freyja's eyes so sharp?" he called to Loke. "They burn me like fire."

"Oh," said the cunning serving-maid, "she has not slept for a week, so anxious has she been to come here, and that is why her eyes are so fiery."

Everybody looked at the bride and nobody envied Thrym. They thought it was too much like marrying a thunder-storm.

The giant's sister came into the hall just then, and seeing the veiled form of the bride sitting there went up to her and asked for a bridal gift. "If you would have my love and friendship give me those rings of gold upon your fingers."

But the bride sat perfectly silent. No one had yet seen her face or heard her voice.

Thrym became very impatient. "Bring in the hammer," he shouted, "that the bride may be consecrated, and wed us in the name of Var."

If the giant could have seen the bride's eyes when she heard these words he would have sent her home as quickly as possible, and looked somewhere else for a wife.

The hammer was brought and placed in the bride's lap, and everybody looked to see the marriage ceremony; but the wedding was more strange and terrible than the bridal journey had been. No sooner did the bride's fingers close round the handle of Mjolner than the veil which covered her face was torn off and there stood Thor, the giant-queller, his terrible eyes blazing with wrath. The giants shuddered and shrank away from those flaming eyes, the sight of which they dreaded more than anything else in all the worlds; but there was no chance of escape. Thor swung the hammer round his head and the great house rocked on its foundations. There was a vivid flash of lightning, an awful crash of thunder, and the burning roof and walls buried the whole company in one common ruin.

Thrym was punished for stealing the hammer, his wedding guests got crushing blows instead of bridal gifts, and Thor and Loke went back to Asgard, where the presence of Mjolner made the gods safe once more.

XI. How Thor fought the Giant Hrungner

One bright summer morning, Thor, the God of Thunder, rode out of Asgard far eastward, fighting giants as he went and slaying them with his mighty hammer, Mjolner; but Odin, his beautiful blue mantle shining with stars and his helmet of gold glittering in the clear air, mounted his swift horse Sleipner, and went to Jotunheim, the home of the greatest giant of them all. As he swept along every one stopped to look, for such a horse and such a rider were rarely seen on earth. Sometimes the swift hoofs clattered along the rocky roads across the open country, sometimes they struck quick echoes out of the mountain sides in the deep dells, sometimes they rang along the very summits of the hills; and again, in an instant, horse and rider swept noiseless through the air like a strange phantom in the clear mid-day.

When Odin reached Jotunheim he came upon Hrungner, the strongest of the giants.

"Who are you, riding through air with golden helmet and flowing mantle?" asked the giant. "You have a splendid horse."

"None half so good in Jotunheim!" was Odin's answer.

Odin's boast made the giant angry. "None half so good?" he repeated. "I'll show you a better myself."

Whereupon he sprang on Goldfax and off they both went like a rushing wind. Neither gods nor men ever saw such a race before as these ran over earth and through air, Sleipner dashing with foaming flanks ahead and Goldfax close behind with flaming eye and mane outspread. So eager was the chase and so full of rage and desire the mind of Hrungner that before he knew it he was carried within the gates of Asgard, where the welcome of the gods, as they gathered round the foaming chargers, almost made him forget that he was among his enemies.

They led him into the great hall where the feasts were held, and after their usual manner set out the great tankards brimming with wine, and filled for him the hollow horns from which Thor often drank deep and long. As they were set before him the giant drained them one by one at a single draught; and after a time, as horn after horn of sparkling wine was poured down Hrungner's capacious throat, he forgot his peril, and after the manner of drunken men began to boast of his mighty deeds and of the terrible things he meant to do against the gods.

"Oho," he shouted, "I'll pick up this little Valhal in one hand and carry it off to Jotunheim; I'll pull this high-walled Asgard down stone after stone, and knock the heads of all these puny gods together until none are left save Freyja and Sif, and they shall boil my pot and keep my house for me." And so this drunken giant disturbed the peace of heaven, and the gods were sorry enough that he had ever ridden within their gates, but he was their guest, and the rites of hospitality must be respected even with a drunken braggart. So Freyja filled his horn again and again, until he roared out in a drunken fury, "I'll drink every drop of wine in Asgard before I leave."

This boast made the gods, already weary of his boasting, indignant, and they called on Thor to rid them of the braggart. The God of Thunder came striding into the hall swinging his mighty hammer, with anger on his brow and in his eye, to hear the gods insulted under the very roof of Asgard.

"Why does this stupid giant sit here in Asgard drinking our wine as if he were a god?" shouted Thor, glaring at Hrungner as if he would smite him on the spot; but Hrungner, full of drunken courage, glared back at Thor.

"I came here with Odin," he growled, "and the hospitality of the gods will suffer more than I if a hand is laid on me."

"You may rue that hospitality before you are out of Asgard," was the angry reply of Thor.

"Small honour to you if you slay me here unarmed and solitary; if you want to prove your boasted valour meet me face to face at Grjottungard. Foolish it was in me to leave my shield and flint-stone at home; had I those weapons I would challenge you to fight me here and now, but if you kill me unarmed I proclaim you a coward in the face of all Asgard."

"I will meet you, braggart, when and where you will," hotly retorted Thor, whom no giant had ever before challenged to a *holmgang*, or single combat. And Hrungner got himself safely out of Asgard and journeyed as fast as he could to Jotunheim to make ready for the fight.

When the news of these things spread there was nothing heard of among the giants but Hrungner's journey and the *holmgang* he was to fight with Thor. Nobody thought or talked of anything else, for if Hrungner, the most powerful of them all, should be beaten, Thor would never cease to make war upon them. Long and earnest was the talk among the giants, for Thor's terrible hammer had often rung among the hills, and they dreaded the flash of it through the air and the crash of it as it fell smiting and crushing whatsoever opposed it. To give Hrungner courage they built an immense giant of clay at Grjottungard, but they could find no heart big enough for such a huge body, and so they were obliged at last to use a mare's heart, which fluttered and throbbed terribly when Thor came; for it is the heart and not the size of the body which makes one strong and great. The clay giant, when finished, was so vast that the shadow of him was like a cloud upon the landscape. When all was ready Hrungner stood beside the false giant ready for the fight, and a terrible foe he was, too; for his heart was as hard as rock, his head was of stone, and so was the great broad shield he held before him. And swung on his shoulder was the huge flint-stone which he meant to hurl at Thor.

Thor meanwhile was on his way to Grjottungard with his servant Thjalfe, and Thjalfe ran ahead, and when he saw Hrungner, called out, "You stand unguarded, giant; you hold your shield before you, and Thor has seen you, and will come violently upon you from beneath the earth."

Then Hrungner threw his shield on the ground and stood upon it, grasping the flint-stone in both hands.

In a moment the sky began to darken with rushing clouds, broad flashes of lightning blazed across the heavens, and deafening peals of thunder rolled crashing over the terror-stricken earth. Striding from cloud to cloud, swinging his terrible hammer in an awful uproar of lightning and storm, Thor came rushing on in all his god-like might. The heavens were on fire, the mountains shook on their foundations, and the earth rocked to and fro as the god of strength moved on to battle.

Poor Mokkerkalfe, the clay giant, was so frightened that the perspiration poured in streams from his great body, and his cowardly heart fluttered like an imprisoned bird. Then Thor, swinging the flashing hammer with all his might, hurled it at Hrungner, and on the very instant the giant flung the flint-stone. The two rushed like meteors and met with a tremendous crash in mid-air. The flint-stone broke in pieces, one falling to the ground and making a mountain where it lay, and the other striking Thor with such force that he fell full-length on the ground; but the terrible hammer struck Hrungner in the very centre of his forehead, crushed his head into small pieces, and threw him with his foot across Thor's neck. Thjalfe meanwhile had thrown himself on Mokkerkalfe, and the clay giant, like a great many other sham giants, fell into pieces at the very first blow; and so Thor was victor of the *holmgang*.

But how was Thor to get up? The dead giant's foot lay across his neck, and, try as he might with all his strength, he could not lift it off. Then Thjalfe came and tried in vain to set Thor free; and when the gods heard of the trouble Thor was in they all came, and one by one tried to lift Hrungner's foot, and not one of them could do it; so although Thor had killed the giant it looked as if the giant had beaten him too. After a time Thor's little son Magne, or strength, came that way. He was only three days old, but he walked quickly up to his father, quietly lifted the immense foot and threw it on the ground as if it were the easiest thing in the world, saying as he did so, "It was a great mishap that I came so late, father; for I believe I could have slain this giant with my fist."

Thor rose up quickly and greeted his son as if he were prouder of him than of the slaying of the giant, and declared that he should have the giant's beautiful horse Goldfax for a reward; but Odin would not listen to it, and so Magne had to content himself with his father's praise and the glory of his wonderful deed.

Even now Thor's troubles were not ended, for the piece of flint-stone which struck his head so violently that it threw him to the ground remained imbedded in it, and made the strong god so much trouble that when he had reached Thrudvang, or thunder-world, he sent for the sorceress Groa, the wife of the wise Orvandel, that she might remove the unwieldy stone. Groa came with all her wisdom and began weaving magic spells about Thor, and singing strange incantations to the most weird and mysterious airs in the world, until the flint-stone became entirely loose. When he felt the stone gradually loosened, and knew that Groa could take it out in a moment, Thor was so glad that he tried to think how he might reward her in some way for the good service she had done him; and as even a god cannot give anything greater than happiness, he bethought himself of something which would make her very happy. So he began to speak of Orvandel, who had long been absent from her, and whom she greatly loved. He told her that he had entered Jotunheim from the north, wading the deep rivers, and had secreted Orvandel in a basket, and so borne him out of the giant's country, and that as they journeyed along in the bitter weather one of Orvandel's toes protruded from the basket and was frozen, and he, Thor, broke it off and threw it into the shining sky, where it had become the star called "Orvandel's Toe"; and then he added that Orvandel would shortly come to his home again.

When Groa heard this news of her husband she was filled with such joy that all her magical songs and wonderful incantations went straight out of her head and she could not get them back again, and the stone remains in Thor's head to this day. And this is the reason why no one must ever throw a flint-stone across the floor, because when this happens the stone in Thor's head moves, and the strong god is very uncomfortable.

XII. The Binding of the Wolf

Loke looked like a god and had many of the wonderful gifts which the gods possessed, but at heart he was one of those giants who were always trying to cross Bifrost, the shining rainbow-bridge, at the heavenly end of which Heimdal kept guard day and night, with eyes so keen that in the darkness as easily as in the light he could see a hundred miles distant, and with ears so sharp that he could hear the noiseless blossoming of the grass in the deepest valley, and the growing of the wool upon the backs of sheep browsing along the hill-tops. Loke had the mind of the gods, who were always working to bring order and beauty into the world, but he had the heart of the giants, who were striving to undo the good and cover the earth with howling storms and icy desolation. After he had been in Asgard for a time he wanted to get back to Jotunheim, where his true home was. There he married a terrible giantess, and three children were born to him more repulsive than their mother,—Hel, the Midgard-serpent, and the Fenris-wolf. These monsters grew to be very strong and horrible to look upon before the gods thought of destroying them; but one day, as Odin looked over the worlds from his throne, a shadow fell upon his face, for he saw how powerful the children of Loke were becoming, and he knew they would work endless mischief and misery for gods and men; so he sent some of the gods to bring the monsters to Asgard. It was a strange sight when Loke's children were brought into heaven,—Hel's terrible face turning into stone every one who looked, unless he were a god; the Midgard-serpent coiling its immense length into great circles over which the glittering eyes wandered restlessly; and the Fenris-wolf growling with a deep, cruel voice. Odin looked sternly at Loke, the evil god who had brought such savage beings among men, and then with a dark brow he cast Hel down into the dusky kingdoms of the dead, and hurled the snake into the deep sea, where he grew until he coiled around the whole earth; but Fenrer, the wolf, was permitted to grow up in Asgard. He was so fierce that only Tyr, the sword-god, could feed him. He roamed about Asgard, his huge body daily growing stronger, and his hungry eyes flashing more and more fiercely.

After a time another shadow fell upon Odin's face, for Fenrer was fast becoming the most terrible enemy of the gods, and the oracles who could look into the future, said that at the last great battle he would destroy Odin himself. So Odin called all the gods together, and as they came into the great hall the wolf crouched at the door, with a look that made even their strong hearts shudder.

"Our most dangerous enemy is growing stronger every day under our roof and by our hands," said Odin, "and we shall cease to be gods if we are so blind as to nourish our own destroyer."

"Kill him!" muttered some one.

"No," said Odin; "although he is to devour me, no blood shall stain the sacred seats of the gods."

"Chain him!" said Thor.

That was a good plan, they all agreed, but how was it to be done?

"Leave that to me," answered Thor, full of courage, for he had done many wonderful things, and there was nothing of which he was afraid.

That night the fires in the great smithy blazed and roared so fiercely that the heavens far around were lighted with the glow, and in the dusky light the strong forms of the gods moved to and fro as they worked on the chain with which they meant to bind the Fenris-wolf. All night Thor's mighty strokes rang on the hard iron, and when the morning came the chain was done, and they called it Leding. Then the gods called Fenrer, spread out the chain, and asked him to show his wonderful strength by breaking it.

The wolf knew better than the gods how strong he had grown, and that the breaking of Leding would be a very small matter for him; so he permitted them to bind the great links around his shaggy body and about his feet, and to rivet the ends so fast that it seemed as if nothing on earth could ever break them apart again. When it was all done, and Thor's eyes were beginning to smile at his success, the wolf got quietly upon his feet, stretched himself as easily as if a web of silk were cast over him, snapped the massive chain in a dozen places, and walked off, leaving the gods to gather up the broken links.

"He has grown terribly strong," said Odin, looking at the great pieces of iron.

"Yes," answered sturdy Thor, "stronger than I thought; but I will forge another chain, which even he cannot break."

Again the red glow shone in the sky over Asgard, the fires flashed and blazed, and the great hammers rang far into the night, and the next day the mighty chain Drome, twice as strong as Leding, was finished.

"Come, Fenrer," said Thor, "you are already famous for your strength; but if you can break this chain no one will ever be able to deny your strength, and you will win great honour among gods and men."

The wolf growled as he looked at the great chain, for he knew that the gods feared him and wanted to make him harmless. He knew also that he could break the chain which they had forged with so much toil to bind him with, and so he let them fasten him as before. When all was done, the gods began to smile again, for they had made the strongest chain that ever was or could be made, and now surely the wolf was forever harmless.

But Fenrer knew better than they. He rose slowly, with the massive links bound closely about him, shook himself fiercely, stretched himself, and then with a mighty effort dashed himself on the ground; the earth shook, the chain burst, and its links flew through the air and buried themselves in the ground, so tremendous was the effort with which the wolf freed himself. A fierce joy gleamed in his eyes as he walked away with deep growls, leaving the gods to console themselves as best they might, for there were no more chains to be made.

Long and anxiously they talked together, but no one could think of anything which could hold Fenrer until Odin called to Skirner, Frey's swiftest messenger: "Go to Svartalfheim as fast as the flash of Thor's hammer, and the dwarfs shall make us an enchanted chain which even he cannot break."

Skirner was off almost before Odin had done speaking. Travelling over land and sea he soon came to the dark entrance of the under-world where the dwarfs lived, and in a very short time he was in the dusky home of the wonderful little workers in iron. They were rushing about with black faces and dirty hair when Skirner called them together and said, "You must make for the gods an enchanted chain so slight that Fenrer will be willing to be bound by it, and so strong that when he has allowed himself to be tied he cannot break loose again."

The dwarfs whispered together for a few moments, and then scattered in every direction; for they were going to make the most wonderful chain that was ever put together, and there were many things to be looked after before it could be done. Skirner sat in the darkness until the busy little workers had finished the band, and then he carried it quickly to Asgard, where all the gods were waiting anxiously for his coming and Fenrer was stealthily stealing from place to place through the city. Skirner spread the string out for the gods to look at, and they could hardly believe it was strong enough. It was very long, but so small and soft that it seemed no more than silken twine; it was made out of such things as the sound of a cat's footsteps, the roots of the mountains, the breath of a fish, and the sinews of a bear, and nothing could break it.

The gods were so happy in the hope of being relieved of their enemy that they could not thank Skirner enough. They all went to a rocky island in a lake called Amsvartner, taking the wolf with them. Thor showed the silken twine to Fenrer. "You have broken Leding and Drome," he said, "and now you will break this also, although it is somewhat stronger than one would think, to look at it."

Then he handed the magic cord from one god to another and each tried to break it, but no one succeeded.

"We cannot do it," they all said after it had been handed around the circle, "but Fenrer can."

The wolf looked at it suspiciously.

"It is such a slender thread," he answered, "that I shall get no credit if I break it; and if it is made with magic, slight as it looks I shall never get loose from it again."

The gods looked at one another and smiled.

"Oh, you will easily break so slim a band as that," they replied, "since you have already broken the heaviest chains in the world; and if you cannot break it we will loosen you again."

"If you bind me so fast that I am not able to get myself free, I shall get little help from you," said the wolf truthfully enough. "I am very unwilling to have this twine bound about me; but that you may not be able to call me cowardly, I will do it if some one of you will lay his hand in my mouth as a pledge that there is no deceit about this thing."

The gods looked at each other when they heard these words. Fenrer had spoken the truth, there was no denying that. He must be chained now, however, or they would all be destroyed; but who would lose a hand to save the rest? Thor's hands were needed to swing the hammer against the giants, and everybody could think of some very good reason why his hand should not be lost. There was an awful pause, and then Tyr, the god of honour and courage, who had never stood still when he ought to go forward, stretched out his right hand and laid it in the wolf's hungry mouth.

Then the gods bound the slender cord tightly around Fenrer, fold on fold, winding its whole length about him and tying the ends tightly together. It was so slight that it seemed as if it must break in fifty places as soon as the wolf began to stretch himself. So perhaps thought Fenrer himself; but the harder he strove to break loose, the closer the cord drew about him. He sprang from side to side, he threw himself on the ground, he stretched his mighty limbs with all his strength, but the twine only cut the deeper. Then a mighty rage filled the wolf because he had suffered himself to be deceived, his eyes flamed with fury, and the foam ran out of his mouth. The gods were so delighted when they found the wolf really fast at last that they began to laugh, all except brave Tyr, who lost his right hand.

They took the wonderful silken chain and drew it through the middle of a rock and sunk the rock so deep in the earth that nothing but an earthquake could stir it. Fenrer, wild with pain and rage, rushed from side to side so violently that the earth rocked beneath him, and opening his tremendous jaws sprang upon the gods; whereupon they thrust a sword into his cruel jaws so that the hilt stood on his lower jaw and the point pierced the roof of the mouth.

So the Fenris-wolf was bound and made fast to the rocky island, his jaws spread far apart, foaming and growling until the last great day.

XIII. Thor's Wonderful Journey

Thor made many journeys and had many strange adventures; but there was one journey which was more wonderful than all the others, and which proves, moreover, that the strongest and truest are sometimes deceived by those who are weaker than themselves. The giants in old Norse times were not easy to conquer; but generally it was when they hid themselves behind lies and appeared to be what they were not that they succeeded for a time. Thor's strength was a noble thing because he used it to help men; but his truthfulness and honesty were nobler still.

One morning, just as the sun was beginning to shine through the mists that overhung the world, the gates of Asgard opened and Thor's chariot, drawn by the goats, rattled along the road. Thor and Loke were evidently off for a journey; but Thor was always going off somewhere, and nobody who saw him now thought that he was starting out to try his strength with the most powerful things in the whole earth. Nor did he know it. All day long the chariot rolled across the level stretches of meadow and through the valleys, leaving the echoes shouting to each other from the overhanging mountains as it passed by. At night it stopped at the house of a poor peasant, and Thor stepped down and stood in the doorway.

"Can you lodge two travellers over night?" he asked.

"Certainly," said the peasant, "but we can give you nothing to eat, for we have nothing for ourselves."

"Give yourselves no trouble about that," answered Thor cheerfully; "I can provide for all."

He went back to Loke, who got out of the chariot; and then,

to the great astonishment of the people in the house, Thor killed both his goats, and in a minute they were ready for cooking. The great pot was soon sending savory odours through the house, and the whole family with their strange guests sat down shortly to a bountiful supper.

"The more you eat the better I shall like it," said Thor, as they took their places at the table, "but do not on any account break the bones; when you have done with them throw them into the skins which I have spread out on the hearth."

The peasant and his wife and Thjalfe and Roskva, their two children, ate bountifully; but Thjalfe broke one of the bones to get the marrow. The next morning Thor was up with the sun, and when he dressed himself he took the hammer and held it over the goat-skins: and immediately the bones flew into place, and the skins covered them, and there were the two goats as full of life as when they started out the day before. But one of the goats limped; and when Thor saw it he was so angry that he looked like a thunder-cloud, and his fingers closed so tightly round Mjolner that his knuckles were white. Thjalfe, who had been looking with the rest of the family in speechless wonder, was frightened half out of his wits when he saw Thor's rage, and would have run away if he could. The poor peasant and his wife were equally terrified, and besought Thor that he would not destroy them. Seeing them in such misery Thor's anger died out, and he said he would forgive them, but Thjalfe and Roskva must henceforth be his servants. So taking the two children, and leaving the goats with their parents for safe keeping, Thor and Loke set out again.

Thor had decided to go to Jotunheim, and all the morning they travelled eastward until they reached the shore of the sea. They crossed the wide waters quickly and climbed up on the further shore of Jotunheim. Mists floated over the land, and great rocks rose along the coast so stern and black from the wash of the sea and the fury of storms that they seemed like strong giants guarding their country against the giant-queller. Thor led the way, and they soon entered a deep forest through which they travelled until nightfall, Thjalfe, who was very fleet of foot, carrying the sack of provisions. As night came on they looked about for shelter, and came upon an immense building with a whole side opening into a great room off which they found five smaller rooms. This was just what he wanted, although they could not imagine why any one had built such a house in that lonely place. After supper, weary with the long journey, they were soon in a deep sleep.

Three or four hours went by quietly enough, but about midnight they were suddenly awakened by an awful uproar, which shook the building to its foundations and made the whole earth tremble. Thor called the others and told them to go into the further rooms. Half dead with fright they did so, but Thor stretched himself, hammer in hand, at the wide entrance. As soon as there was light enough to see about him Thor went into the woods, and had gone but a little way when he came upon an enormous giant, fast asleep, and snoring so loudly that the very trees shook around him. Thor quickly buckled on his belt of strength, and had no sooner done so than the giant awoke and sprang to his feet. The whole earth shook under him, and he towered as far over Thor, as a great oak does over the fern that grows at its foot. Thor was never frightened, but he had never heard of such a giant before and he looked at him with honest surprise.

"Who are you?" he said, after looking up to the great face a minute.

"I am Skrymer," answered the giant, "but I don't need to ask your name. You are Thor. But what have you done with my glove?"

And stretching out his great hand the giant picked up his glove, which was nothing less than the building Thor and the others had spent the night in.

"Would you like to have me travel with you?" continued the giant.

"Certainly," said Thor, although it was plainly to be seen that neither Thjalfe nor Roskva wanted such a companion. Skrymer thereupon untied his sack and took out his breakfast, and the others followed his example, taking care, however, to put a comfortable distance between themselves and their dangerous fellow-traveller. After breakfast Skrymer proposed that they should put all their provisions into one bag, to which Thor consented, and they started off, the giant tramping on ahead, and carrying the sack on his broad back.

All day long he walked steadily on, taking such tremendous strides that the others could hardly keep up with him. When night came he stopped under a great oak.

"There," said he, throwing down the sack; "take that and get some supper; I am going to sleep."

The words were hardly out of his mouth before he began to snore as loudly as the night before. Thor took the sack, but the harder he tried to loosen the string the tighter it drew, and with all his strength he could not untie a single knot. Finding he could not get into the sack, and hearing the giant snore so peacefully at his side, Thor's anger blazed out, and grasping the hammer he struck the giant full on the head. Skrymer opened his eyes drowsily.

"Did a leaf fall on my head?" he called out sleepily, without getting up. "Have you had your supper yet, and are you going to bed?"

In a minute he was snoring again. Thor went and lay down under another oak; but at midnight the giant began to snore so heavily that the forest resounded with the noise. Thor was fairly beside himself with rage, and swinging his hammer struck Skrymer such a tremendous blow that the hammer sank to the handle in his head. The giant opened his eyes and sat up.

"What is the matter now?" he called out; "did an acorn fall on my head? How are you getting on, Thor?"

"Oh, I am just awake," said Thor, stepping back quickly. "It is only midnight, and we may sleep awhile longer."

Thor watched until the giant had fallen asleep again, and just at daybreak dealt him the most terrible blow that he had ever given with the hammer. It flashed through and buried itself out of sight in Skrymer's forehead. The giant sprang on his feet and began to stroke his beard.

"Are there any birds up there?" he asked, looking into the oak. "I thought a feather dropped on my head. Are you awake, Thor? It is full time to dress, and you are near the end of your journey. The city of Utgard is not far off. I heard you whispering together that I was a man of great stature, but you will find much larger men in Utgard. Take my advice, and when you get there don't boast very much, for they will not take boasting from such little fellows as you are. You would do well to turn back and go home while you have a chance; but if you will go on, take the road to the eastward,—my way takes me to the north." And, swinging the sack of provisions over his shoulder, Skrymer plunged into the forest and was soon out of sight.

Thor and his companions pushed on as fast as they could until noon, when suddenly a great city rose before them, on a vast plain, the walls of which were so high that they had to lean back as far as they could to see the top. A great gate, heavily barred, stopped them at the entrance; but they crept between the bars. After going a little distance they came upon a palace, and the doors being open went in, and found themselves in a great hall with long seats on either side, and on these seats rows of gigantic men larger than Skrymer. When they saw Utgard-Loke, who was the king of that country, they saluted him; but he sat for a long time without taking any notice of them. At last smiling contemptuously he said: "It is tiresome for travellers to be asked about a long journey; but if I am not mistaken this little fellow is Thor. Perhaps, however, you are really larger than you seem to be. What feats of strength can you show us? No one is permitted to stay here unless he excels in some difficult thing."

Hearing these words, in a very insulting tone, Loke answered loudly, "There is one feat in which no one can equal me, and I am ready to perform it at once. I can devour food faster than any one here."

"Truly, that would be a feat if you could do it," said the scornful king; and he called to a man named Loge to contend with Loke.

A great trough full of meat was placed in the centre of the hall, and commencing at either end the contestants began to eat voraciously, and so fast that it is disagreeable even to think of it. They reached the middle of the trough at exactly the same moment; but Loke had eaten only the meat, while Loge had devoured meat, bones, trough and all. There was nothing left on his side, and Loke had to confess himself beaten.

Then the king, looking at Thjalfe, asked, "What can you do, young man?"

"I will run a race with any one you will select," answered Thjalfe promptly.

"If you can outrun any one I can select, it will certainly be a splendid feat," said Utgard-Loke; "but you must be very swift-footed to do it."

There was a noble race-ground just outside the palace, and every one hurried out to see the race. The king called a slender young fellow named Huge, and told him to run with Thjalfe.

There was never such running since the world began. Thjalfe ran like the wind; but Huge reached the goal first, and turned about to meet Thjalfe as he came breathless to the post.

"You must use your legs better than that if you intend to win," said the king, as Thjalfe walked back; "although you are the fastest runner that ever came here."

They ran a second time, but when Huge reached the goal and turned around, Thjalfe was a full bow-shot behind.

"Well run!" shouted Utgard-Loke; "well run! a third race shall decide it."

A third time they were at the starting-place and again they were speeding down the course, while everybody strained his eyes to look at them; and a third time Huge reached the goal and turned to find Thjalfe not half-way.

"We have had racing enough!" cried the giants, and they all went back into the palace again.

And now it was Thor's turn to show his wonderful strength; but he did not dream that he was going to measure strength with the most tremendous forces in the whole earth.

"Your fame fills all the worlds, Thor," called out Utgard-Loke, when they had seated themselves on the benches along the great hall; "give us some proof of your wonderful power."

Thor never waited to be asked a second time.

"I will contend in drinking with any one you may select," was his prompt acceptance of the challenge.

"Well answered," said the king. "Bring out the great horn."

A giant went out, and speedily came back bearing a very deep horn, which the king said his men were compelled to empty as a punishment.

"A good drinker will empty that horn at a single draught," said Utgard-Loke, as it was filled and handed to Thor; "a few men need to drink twice, but only a milksop needs a third pull at it."

Thor thought the horn not over large, although very long, and as he was very thirsty he put it to his lips without further ado, and drank so long and deep that he thought it certainly must be empty, but when he set the horn down and looked into it he was astonished to find that the liquor rose almost as high as when he set his lips to it.

"That was fairly well drunk," said the king, "but not unusually so; if anybody had told me Thor could do no better than that I would not have believed him. But of course you will finish it at a second draught."

Thor said nothing, although he was very angry, but setting the horn to his lips a second time he drank longer and deeper than before. When he had stopped to take breath, and looked at it again, he had drunk less than the first time.

"How now, Thor," cried Utgard-Loke, "you have left more for the third draught than you can manage. If there are no other feats which you can perform better than this you must not expect to be considered as great here as among the gods."

Thor became very angry when he heard these words, and seizing the horn he drank deep, fast, and furiously until he thought it certainly must be empty; but when he looked into it the liquor had fallen so little that he could hardly see the difference; and he handed it to the cupbearer, and would drink no more.

"It is plain," spoke up the king in a very insulting tone, "that you are not so strong as we thought you were; you cannot succeed in this strife, certainly; will you try something else?"

"I will certainly try something else," said Thor, who could not understand why he had failed to drain the horn; "but I am sure that even among the gods such draughts would not be counted small. What game do you propose now?"

"Oh, a very easy one," replied the king, "which my youngsters here make nothing of; simply to lift a cat from the floor. I should not think of asking you to try it if I did not see that you are much less of a man than I have always supposed."

He had no sooner said this than a large grey cat ran out into the hall. Thor put his hand under it and tried to lift it, but the cat arched its back as high as Thor stretched his hands, and, do his best, he could only get one foot off the floor.

"It is just as I expected," cried Utgard-Loke in a loud voice; "the cat is very large, and Thor is a very little fellow compared with the rest of us."

Thor's eyes flashed fire. "Little as I am," he shouted, "I challenge any of you to wrestle with me."

Utgard-Loke looked up and down the benches as if he would call out some one from the two rows of giants. Then he shook his head, saying; "There is no one here who would not think it child's play to wrestle with you; but let some one call in Ellie, my old nurse; she shall try her strength with you. She has brought many a stronger man than you to earth."

An old woman came creeping into the hall, bent, wrinkled, and toothless. Thor seized her, but the tighter his grasp became the firmer she stood. Her thin arms gripped him like a vise, her strength seemed to grow as she put it forth, and at last after a hard struggle, in which Thor strained every muscle to the breaking point, he sank on one knee.

"That is enough," said Utgard-Loke, and the old woman crept feebly out of the hall, leaving Thor stunned and bewildered in the midst of the silent giants. There were no more trials of strength, and Thor and his companions were generously feasted after their defeats.

The next morning, after they had partaken of a bountiful breakfast of meat and drink, they started on their journey homeward. Utgard-Loke went with them as far as the gate of the city, where he stopped.

"How do you think your journey has turned out?" he asked Thor; "and have you met any men stronger than yourself?"

"I have brought shame upon myself," answered Thor frankly and honestly, after his nature, "and it vexes me to think that you will hereafter speak of me as a weak fellow."

"Now that you are out of the city I will tell you the truth about these things," said Utgard-Loke. "If I had known how mighty you are I would never have allowed you to enter the gates, and you may be very sure you will never get in a second time. I have beaten you by deception, not by strength. I have been deluding you from the start. In the forest I tied the sack with a tough iron wire in such a way you could not discern the secret of the knot. Thrice you struck at me with your hammer, and the first blow, though the lightest, would have killed me had it fallen on me; but each time I slipped a mountain between myself and the hammer, and the blows made three deep clefts in its stony sides. I have deluded you, too, in all the trials of strength and skill. Loke was very hungry, and ate voraciously, but he contended against fire itself, which goes like the wind and devours everything in its path; Thjalfe ran as man never ran before, but Huge, who raced with him, was no other than my thought, and what man is so swift as thought? The horn which you strove in vain to empty had its further end in the sea, and so mighty were your draughts that over the wide sea the waters have sunk to the ebb. Your strength was no less wonderful when you lifted the cat; when we saw one foot raised from the floor our hearts sank in terror, for it was the Midgard-serpent, encircling the whole earth, which you really contended against, and you held it aloft so near heaven that the world was hardly enclosed by its folds. Most marvellous of all was the wrestling with Ellie, who was none other than old age itself, who sooner or later must bring all things to the ground. We must part, I hope never to meet again; for I can only defend myself against you by spells of magic such as these."

Thor was so enraged when he heard these words that he swung his hammer high in air to crush the lying Utgard-Loke, but he had vanished, and when Thor turned to look for the city he saw only a beautiful plain spreading its blossoming meadows to the far mountains; and he went thoughtfully back to Asgard.

XIV. The Death of Balder

There was one shadow which always fell over Asgard. Sometimes in the long years the gods almost forgot it, it lay so far off, like a dim cloud in a clear sky; but Odin saw it deepen and widen as he looked out into the universe, and he knew that the last great battle would surely come, when the gods themselves would be destroyed and a long twilight would rest on all the worlds; and now the day was close at hand. Misfortunes never come singly to men, and they did not to the gods. Idun, the beautiful goddess of youth, whose apples were the joy of all Asgard, made a resting place for herself among the massive branches of Ygdrasil, and there every evening came Brage, and sang so sweetly that the birds stopped to listen, and even the Norns, those implacable sisters at the foot of the tree, were softened by the melody. But poetry cannot change the purposes of fate, and one evening no song was heard of Brage or birds, the leaves of the world-tree hung withered and lifeless on the branches, and the fountain from which they had daily been sprinkled was dry at last. Idun had fallen into the dark valley of death, and when Brage, Heimdal, and Loke went to question her about the future she could answer them only with tears. Brage would not leave his beautiful wife alone amid the dim shades that crowded the dreary valley, and so youth and genius vanished out of Asgard forever.

Balder was the most god-like of all the gods, because he was the purest and the best. Wherever he went his coming was like the coming of sunshine, and all the beauty of summer was but the shining of his face. When men's hearts were white like the light, and their lives clear as the day, it was because Balder was looking down upon them with those soft, clear eyes that were open windows to the soul of God. He had always lived in such a glow of brightness that no darkness had ever touched him; but one morning, after Idun and Brage had gone, Balder's face was sad and troubled. He walked slowly from room to room in his palace Breidablik, stainless as the sky when April showers have swept across it because no impure thing had ever crossed the threshold, and his eyes were heavy with sorrow. In the night terrible dreams had broken his sleep, and made it a long torture. The air seemed to be full of awful changes for him, and for all the gods. He knew in his soul that the shadow of the last great day was sweeping on; as he looked out and saw the worlds lying in light and beauty, the fields yellow with waving grain, the deep fiords flashing back the sunbeams from their clear depths, the verdure clothing the loftiest mountains, and knew that over all this darkness and desolation would come, with silence of reapers and birds, with fading of leaf and flower, a great sorrow fell on his heart.

Balder could bear the burden no longer. He went out, called all the gods together, and told them the terrible dreams of the night. Every face was heavy with care. The death of Balder would be like the going out of the sun, and after a long, sad council the gods resolved to protect him from harm by pledging all things to stand between him and any hurt. So Frigg, his mother, went forth and made everything promise, on a solemn oath, not to injure her son. Fire, iron, all kinds of metal, every sort of stone, trees, earth, diseases, birds, beasts, snakes, as the anxious mother went to them, solemnly pledged themselves that no harm should come near Balder. Everything promised, and Frigg thought she had driven away the cloud; but fate was stronger than her love, and one little shrub had not sworn.

Odin was not satisfied even with these precautions, for whichever way he looked the shadow of a great sorrow spread over the worlds. He began to feel as if he were no longer the greatest of the gods, and he could almost hear the rough shouts of the frost-giants crowding the rainbow bridge on their way into Asgard. When trouble comes to men it is hard to bear, but to a god who had so many worlds to guide and rule it was a new and terrible thing. Odin thought and thought until he was weary, but no gleam of light could he find anywhere; it was thick darkness everywhere.

At last he could bear the suspense no longer, and saddling his horse he rode sadly out of Asgard to Niflheim, the home of Hel, whose face was as the face of death itself. As he drew near the gates, a monstrous dog came out and barked furiously, but Odin rode a little eastward of the shadowy gates to the grave of a wonderful prophetess. It was a cold, gloomy place, and the soul of the great god was pierced with a feeling of hopeless sorrow as he dismounted from Sleipner, and bending over the grave began to chant weird songs, and weave magical charms over it. When he had spoken those wonderful words which could waken the dead from their sleep, there was an awful silence for a moment, and then a faint ghost-like voice came from the grave.

"Who art thou?" it said. "Who breaketh the silence of death, and calleth the sleeper out of her long slumbers? Ages ago I was laid at rest here, snow and rain have fallen upon me through myriad years why dost thou disturb me?"

"I am Vegtam," answered Odin, "and I come to ask why the couches of Hel are hung with gold and the benches strewn with shining rings?"

"It is done for Balder," answered the awful voice; "ask me no more."

Odin's heart sank when he heard these words; but he was determined to know the worst.

"I will ask thee until I know all. Who shall strike the fatal blow?"

"If I must, I must," moaned the prophetess. "Hoder shall smite his brother Balder and send him down to the dark home of Hel. The mead is already brewed for Balder, and the despair draweth near."

Then Odin, looking into the future across the open grave, saw all the days to come.

"Who is this," he said, seeing that which no mortal could have seen,—"who is this that will not weep for Balder?"

Then the prophetess knew that it was none other than the greatest of the gods who had called her up.

"Thou art not Vegtam," she exclaimed, "thou art Odin himself, the king of men."

"And thou," answered Odin angrily, "art no prophetess, but the mother of three giants."

"Ride home, then, and exult in what thou hast discovered," said the dead woman. "Never shall my slumbers be broken again until Loke shall burst his chains and the great battle come."

And Odin rode sadly homeward knowing that already Niflheim was making itself beautiful against the coming of Balder.

The other gods meanwhile had become merry again; for had not everything promised to protect their beloved Balder? They even made sport of that which troubled them, for when they found that nothing could hurt Balder, and that all things glanced aside from his shining form, they persuaded him to stand as a target for their weapons; hurling darts, spears, swords, and battle-axes at him, all of which went singing through the air and fell harmless at his feet. But Loke, when he saw these sports, was jealous of Balder, and went about thinking how he could destroy him.

It happened that as Frigg sat spinning in her house Fensal, the soft wind blowing in at the windows and bringing the merry shouts of the gods at play, an old woman entered and approached her.

"Do you know," asked the newcomer, "what they are doing in Asgard? They are throwing all manner of dangerous weapons at Balder. He stands there like the sun for brightness, and against his glory, spears and battle-axes fall powerless to the ground. Nothing can harm him."

"No," answered Frigg joyfully; "nothing can bring him any hurt, for I have made everything in heaven and earth swear to protect him."

"What!" said the old woman, "has everything sworn to guard Balder?"

"Yes," said Frigg, "everything has sworn except one little

shrub which is called Mistletoe, and grows on the eastern side of Valhal. I did not take an oath from that because I thought it too young and weak."

When the old woman heard this a strange light came into her eyes; she walked off much faster than she had come in, and no sooner had she passed beyond Frigg's sight than this same feeble old woman grew suddenly erect, shook off her woman's garments, and there stood Loke himself. In a moment he had reached the slope east of Valhal, had plucked a twig of the unsworn Mistletoe, and was back in the circle of the gods, who were still at their favourite pastime with Balder. Hoder was standing silent and alone outside the noisy throng, for he was blind. Loke touched him.

"Why do you not throw something at Balder?"

"Because I cannot see where Balder stands, and have nothing to throw if I could," replied Hoder.

"If that is all," said Loke, "come with me. I will give you something to throw, and direct your aim."

Hoder, thinking no evil, went with Loke and did as he was told.

The little sprig of Mistletoe shot through the air, pierced the heart of Balder, and in a moment the beautiful god lay dead upon the field. A shadow rose out of the deep beyond the worlds and spread itself over heaven and earth, for the light of the universe had gone out.

The gods could not speak for horror. They stood like statues for a moment, and then a hopeless wail burst from their lips. Tears fell like rain from eyes that had never wept before, for Balder, the joy of Asgard, had gone to Niflheim and left them desolate. But Odin was saddest of all, because he knew the future, and he knew that peace and light had fled from Asgard forever, and that the last day and the long night were hurrying on.

Frigg could not give up her beautiful son, and when her grief had spent itself a little, she asked who would go to Hel and offer her a rich ransom if she would permit Balder to return to Asgard.

"I will go," said Hermod; swift at the word of Odin Sleipner was led forth, and in an instant Hermod was galloping furiously away.

Then the gods began with sorrowful hearts to make ready for Balder's funeral. When the once beautiful form had been arrayed in grave-clothes they carried it reverently down to the deep sea, which lay, calm as a summer afternoon, waiting for its precious burden. Close to the water's edge lay Balder's Ringhorn, the greatest of all the ships that sailed the seas, but when the gods tried to launch it they could not move it an inch. The great vessel creaked and groaned, but no one could push it down to the water. Odin walked about it with a sad face, and the gentle ripple of the little waves chasing each other over the rocks seemed a mocking laugh to him.

"Send to Jotunheim for Hyrroken," he said at last; and a messenger was soon flying for that mighty giantess.

In a little time, Hyrroken came riding swiftly on a wolf so large and fierce that he made the gods think of Fenrer. When the giantess had alighted, Odin ordered four Berserkers of mighty strength to hold the wolf, but he struggled so angrily that they had to throw him on the ground before they could control him. Then Hyrroken went to the prow of the ship and with one mighty effort sent it far into the sea, the rollers underneath bursting into flame, and the whole earth trembling with the shock. Thor was so angry at the uproar that he would have killed the giantess on the spot if he had not been held back by the other gods. The great ship floated on the sea as she had often done before, when Balder, full of life and beauty, set all her sails and was borne joyfully across the tossing seas. Slowly and solemnly the dead god was carried on board, and as Nanna, his faithful wife, saw her husband borne for the last time from the earth which he had made dear to her and beautiful to all men, her heart broke with sorrow, and they laid her beside Balder on the funeral pyre.

Since the world began no one had seen such a funeral. No bells tolled, no long procession of mourners moved across the hills, but all the worlds lay under a deep shadow, and from every quarter came those who had loved or feared Balder. There at the very water's edge stood Odin himself, the ravens flying about his head, and on his majestic face a gloom that no sun would ever lighten again; and there was Frigg, the desolate mother, whose son had already gone so far that he would never come back to her; there was Frey standing sad and stern in his chariot; there was Freyja, the goddess of love, from whose eyes fell a shining rain of tears; there, too, was Heimdal on his horse Goldtop; and around all these glorious ones from Asgard crowded the children of Jotunheim, grim mountain-giants seamed with scars from Thor's hammer, and frost-giants who saw in the death of Balder the coming of that long winter in which they should reign through all the worlds.

A deep hush fell on all created things, and every eye was fixed on the great ship riding near the shore, and on the funeral pyre rising from the deck crowned with the forms of Balder and Nanna. Suddenly a gleam of light flashed over the water; the pile had been kindled, and the flames, creeping slowly at first, climbed faster and faster until they met over the dead and rose skyward. A lurid light filled the heavens and shone on the sea, and in the brightness of it the gods looked pale and sad, and the circle of giants grew darker and more portentous. Thor struck the fast burning pyre with his consecrated hammer, and Odin cast into it the wonderful ring Draupner. Higher and higher leaped the flames, more and more desolate grew the scene; at last they began to sink, the funeral pyre was consumed. Balder had vanished forever, the summer was ended, and winter waited at the doors.

Meanwhile Hermod was riding hard and fast on his gloomy errand. Nine days and nights he rode through valleys so deep and dark that he could not see his horse. Stillness and blackness and solitude were his only companions until he came to the golden bridge which crosses the river Gjol. The good horse Sleipner, who had carried Odin on so many strange journeys, had never travelled such a road before, and his hoofs rang drearily as he stopped short at the bridge, for in front of him stood its porter, the gigantic Modgud.

"Who are you?" she asked, fixing her piercing eyes on Hermod. "What is your name and parentage? Yesterday five bands of dead men rode across the bridge, and beneath them all it did not shake as under your single tread. There is no colour of death in your face. Why ride you hither, the living among the dead?"

"I come," said Hermod, "to seek for Balder. Have you seen him pass this way?"

"He has already crossed the bridge and taken his journey northward to Hel."

Then Hermod rode slowly across the bridge that spans the abyss between life and death, and found his way at last to the barred gates of Hel's dreadful home. There he sprang to the ground, tightened the girths, remounted, drove the spurs deep into the horse, and Sleipner, with a mighty leap, cleared the wall. Hermod rode straight to the gloomy palace, dismounted, entered, and in a moment was face to face with the terrible queen of the kingdom of the dead. Beside her, on a beautiful throne, sat Balder, pale and wan, crowned with a withered wreath of flowers, and close at hand was Nanna, pallid as her husband, for whom she had died. And all night long, while ghostly forms wandered restless and sleepless through Helheim, Hermod talked with Balder and Nanna. There is no record of what they said, but the talk was sad enough, doubtless, and ran like a still stream among the happy days in Asgard when Balder's smile was morning over the earth and the sight of his face the summer of the world.

When the morning came, faint and dim, through the dusky palace, Hermod sought Hel, who received him as cold and stern as fate.

"Your kingdom is full, O Hel!" he said, "and without Balder, Asgard is empty. Send him back to us once more, for there is sadness in every heart and tears are in every eye. Through heaven and earth all things weep for him."

"If that is true," was the slow, icy answer, "if every created thing weeps for Balder, he shall return to Asgard; but if one eye is dry he remains henceforth in Helheim."

Then Hermod rode swiftly away, and the decree of Hel was soon told in Asgard. Through all the worlds the gods sent messengers to say that all who loved Balder should weep for his return, and everywhere tears fell like rain. There was weeping in Asgard, and in all the earth there was nothing that did not weep. Men and women and little children, missing the light that had once fallen into their hearts and homes, sobbed with bitter grief; the birds of the air, who had sung carols of joy at the gates of the morning since time began, were full of sorrow; the beasts of the fields crouched and moaned in their desolation; the great trees, that had put on their robes of green at Balder's command, sighed as the wind wailed through them; and the sweet flowers, that waited for Balder's footstep and sprang up in all the fields to greet him, hung their frail blossoms and wept bitterly for the love and the warmth and the light that had gone out. Throughout the whole earth there was nothing but weeping, and the sound of it was like the wailing of those storms in autumn that weep for the dead summer as its withered leaves drop one by one from the trees.

The messengers of the gods went gladly back to Asgard, for everything had wept for Balder; but as they journeyed they came upon a giantess, called Thok, and her eyes were dry.

"Weep for Balder," they said.

"With dry eyes only will I weep for Balder," she answered. "Dead or alive, he never gave me gladness. Let him stay in Helheim."

When she had spoken these words a terrible laugh broke from her lips, and the messengers looked at each other with pallid faces, for they knew it was the voice of Loke.

Balder never came back to Asgard, and the shadows deepened over all things, for the night of death was fast coming on.

XV. How Loke was Punished

In the beginning Loke had been the brother of Odin, and one of the foremost of the gods, but the lawlessness and passion that were in him had won the mastery, and in earth and heaven he was fast bringing ruin and sorrow. What the hard-hearted frost-giants had always tried to do and failed, Loke did; for in the end the evil in him destroyed Asgard, and brought in the long winter of storm and darkness. It was he who stole Sif's hair and Freyja's necklace, who persuaded Idun to go into the woods that the giant Thjasse might carry off her apples, who stung the dwarf so that the handle of Thor's hammer was shortened, who induced Thor to go on his dangerous journey to Geirrod; but worst of all his crimes was the killing of Balder, and the refusal to weep for him when all the world was in tears.

After bringing so much sorrow upon others, suffering at last came to him. Not long after Balder's death the sea-god Aeger gave a great feast, and brewed ale for the gods in the great kettle which Thor had taken from the giant Hymer. All the gods were there save Thor, and they tried to be merry, although they were sad enough at heart. In the midst of them sat Loke, gloomy and silent, as if his terrible crime had drawn a black line around him. The feast went on merrily; but he seemed to have no part in it, for no one spoke to him. Great horns of ale passed from hand to hand, and as they talked and feasted the gods forgot for a moment the sorrow that lay upon all the world.

"Aeger," said one, "these are good servants of yours. They are quick of eye and foot, and one lacks nothing under their care."

Loke was so full of rage that he could not endure that even

the servants of the other gods should be praised, and with flashing eyes and a face black with hate he sprang from his place and struck the servant nearest him so violently that he fell dead on the floor. A silence of horror fell on all the gods at this new sin, and then with fierce indignation they drove him out, and shut the doors against him forever. Loke strode off furiously for a little distance, and then turned and came back. The gods meantime had become merry again.

"What are they talking about?" he asked another servant who was standing without.

"They are telling their great deeds," answered the servant; "but no one has anything good to say of you."

Maddened by these words, Loke forgot his fear in a terrible rage, strode back into the hall and stood there like a thundercloud; when the gods saw him they became suddenly silent.

"I have travelled hither from a long distance," said he hoarsely, "and I am thirsty; who will give me to drink of the mead?"

No one spoke or stirred. Loke's face grew blacker.

"Why are you all silent?" he cried; "have you lost your tongues? Will you find place for me here, or do you turn me away?"

Brage looked at him steadily and fearlessly. "The gods will never more make room for you," he said.

When he heard these words, Loke ceased to look like a god, for the fury and hate of a devil were in his face. He cursed the gods until every face was pale with horror. Like an accusing conscience he told them all their faults and sins; he made them feel their weaknesses so keenly that Vidar, the silent god, rose to give him his seat and silence him, but now that his fury was let loose nothing could stop him. One by one he called each god by his name, and dragged his weaknesses into the view of all, and last of all he came to Sif, Thor's wife, and cursed her; and now a low muttering was heard afar off, and then a distant roll of thunder deepening into awful peals that echoed and re-echoed among the hills. The gods sat silent in their places, and even Loke grew dumb. Great flashes of lightning flamed through the hall, and made his dark face more terrible to look at. Crash followed close upon crash until the mountains quaked, and the great hall trembled; then came a blinding flash, and Thor stood in the midst swinging Mjolner, and looking as if he would smite the world into fragments. He looked at Loke, and Loke, cowering before Thor's terrible eyes of fire, walked out of the hall cursing Aeger as he went, and wishing that flames might break upon his realm and devour it and him.

And now Loke, no longer a god in nature or in rank, became an outcast and a fugitive flying from the wrath of the gods whom he had insulted and wronged. He went from place to place until he came upon a deep valley among the mountains, so entirely shut in that he thought no one from Asgard could ever look into it. There he built a house in the hollows of the rocks, with four doors through which he could look in every direction, so that no one could come near his hiding-place without his knowing it. He took on many disguises; often in the daytime he took the shape of a salmon and hid in the deep waters, where he floated solitary and motionless while the gods were searching for him far and wide.

Days and weeks passed away, and Loke began to think he was safe from the pursuit of his enemies. He began to busy and amuse himself as he used to do before he was shut out of Asgard. He had always been a skilful fisherman, and now, as he sat alone in his house before the fire, he took flax and yarn and began to knit the meshes of the first net that was made since the world began. His eyes burnt at the thought of the new sport which he was going to have, and his cunning hand wove thread after thread into the growing web. Odin, looking down from his lofty throne, saw the busy weaver, and quickly calling Thor, the strongest, and Kvaser, the keenest of the gods, was soon on the journey to Loke's home among the mountains. Loke was so busy with his net that he did not see them until they were close at hand; then he sprang up, threw the net into the fire, and running to the river changed himself into a salmon, and dove deep into the still waters. When the gods entered the house Loke was nowhere to be found, but the sharp-eyed Kvaser found the half-burnt net among the glowing embers. He pulled it out and held it before Odin and Thor.

"I know what it is," he said in a moment; "it is a net for

fishing; Loke was always a fisherman." Then, as if the thought had suddenly come to him, he added, "He has changed himself into a fish and is hiding in that river."

Odin and Thor were rejoiced to find their enemy so close at hand, and they all began to work on the half-burnt net and quickly finished it. Then they went softly down to the water, threw it in, and drew it slowly up the stream from shore to shore. But Loke swam between two large stones in the bed of the stream and the net only grazed him as it passed over. The gods finding the net empty hung a great stone on it, and, going back to the starting place, drew it slowly up stream again. Never, since the beginning of things, had there been such fishing before! The noisy river rolled swiftly down to the sea, the steep mountains rose on either side and shut out the sun so that even at mid-day it was like twilight. When Loke saw the net coming a second time and found that he could not escape, he waited until it was close at hand, and then with a mighty leap shot over it and plunged into a waterfall just where the river rushed into the sea.

The gods saw the great fish leap into the air and fall into the water, and they instantly turned around and dragged the net toward the sea, Thor wading after it in the middle of the stream. As the net came nearer and nearer Loke saw that he must either swim out into the sea or leap back again over the net. He waited until the shadow of the net was over him, and then with a mighty leap shot into the air and over the net; but Thor was watching, and his strong hand closed round the shining fish. Loke managed to slip through Thor's fingers, but Thor held him by the tail, and that, as the story goes, is the reason why the salmon's tail is so thin and pointed.

Then the gods, glad at heart that they had caught the slayer of Balder, changed Loke into his natural shape and dragged him to a cavern in the mountains near at hand, where they fastened three great rocks, having pierced them first with holes. Loke's two fierce sons, Vale and Nare, they also seized, and changed Vale into a wolf, and immediately he sprang upon his brother and devoured him. Then the gods bound Loke, hand and foot, to the great stones, with iron fetters, and, to make his punishment the more terrible, they hung a serpent over him, which moment by moment through ages and ages dropped poison on his face. Loke's wife, Sigyn, when she saw his agony, stood beside him and caught the venom in a cup, as it fell drop by drop; but when the cup was full and she turned to empty it the poison fell on Loke, and he writhed so terribly that the whole earth trembled and quaked. So Loke was punished, and so he lay, chained and suffering, until the last great battle set him free.

XVI. The Twilight of the Gods

Although Loke was bound, and could do no more harm, Balder could not come back; and so Asgard was no longer the heaven it used to be. The gods were there, but the sunshine and the summer had somehow lost their glory, and were thenceforth pale and faint. At last there came a winter such as neither man nor god had ever seen before. The days were short and dark, blinding storms followed fast upon each other and left mountains of snow behind, fierce winds swept the sky and troubled the sea, and the bitter air froze the very hearts of men into sullen despair. The deepest rivers were fast bound, the fiercest animals died in their lairs, there was no warmth in the sun, and even the icy brightness of the stars was dimmed by drifting snow. The whole earth was buried in a winter so bitter that the gods shivered in Asgard.

The long nights and the short, dark days followed fast upon each other, and as the time drew near when summer would come again men's hearts grew light with hope once more. Each day they looked into the sullen skies, through which clouds of snow were whirling, and said to each other, "To-morrow the summer will come"; but when the morrow came no summer came with it. And all through the months that in other days had been beautiful with flowers the snow fell steadily, and the cold winds blew fiercely, while eyes grew sad and hearts heavy with waiting for a summer that did not come. And it never came again; for this was the terrible Fimbul-winter, long foretold, from which even the gods could not escape. In Jotunheim there was joy among the frost-giants as they shouted to each other through the howling storms, "The Fimbul-winter has come at last." At first men shuddered as they whispered, "Can it be the Fimbul-winter?" But when they knew it beyond all doubting a blind despair filled them, and they were reckless alike of good or evil. Over the whole earth war followed fast upon war, and everywhere there were wrangling and fighting and murder. It hardly snowed fast enough to cover the blood-stains. Mothers forgot to love their little children, and brothers struck each other down as if they were the bitterest enemies.

Three years passed without one breath of the warm south wind or the blossoming of a single flower, and three other years darker and colder succeeded them. A savage joy filled the hearts of the frost-giants, and they shook their clenched hands at Asgard as if they had mastered the gods at last. On the earth there was nothing but silence and despair, and among the gods only patient waiting for the end. One day, as the sun rose dim and cold, a deep howl echoed through the sky, and a great wolf sprang up from the under-world and leaped vainly after it. All day long, through the frosty air, that terrible cry was heard, and all day the giant wolf ran close behind, slowly gaining in the chase. At last, as the sun went down over the snow-covered mountains, the wolf, with a mighty spring, reached and devoured it. The glow upon the hills went out in blackness; it was the last sunset. Faint and colourless the moon rose, and another howl filled the heavens as a second wolf sprang upon her track, ran swiftly behind, and devoured her also. Then came an awful darkness over all as, one by one, the stars fell from heaven, and blackness and whirling snow wrapped all things in their folds. The end had come; the last great battle was to be fought; Ragnarok, the Twilight of the Gods, was at hand.

Suddenly a strange sound broke in upon the darkness and was heard throughout all the worlds; on a lofty height the eagle Egder struck his prophetic harp. The earth shook, mountains crumbled, rocks were rent, and all fetters were broken. Loke shook off his chains and rushed out of his cavern, his heart hot with hate and burning with revenge, the terrible Fenris-wolf broke loose, and out of the deep sea the Midgard-serpent drew his long folds toward the land, lashing the water into foam as he passed. From every quarter the enemies of the gods gathered for the last great battle on the plain of Vigrid, which was a hundred miles wide on each side. Thither came the Fenris-wolf, his hungry jaws stretched so far apart that they reached from earth to heaven; the Midgard-serpent, with fiery eyes and pouring out floods of venom; the awful host of Hel with Loke at their head; the grim ranks of the frost-giants marching behind Hrym; and, last of all, the glittering fire-giants of Muspelheim, the fire-world, with Surt at the front.

The long line of enemies already stretched across the plain when Heimdal, standing on the rainbow bridge, blew the Gjallar-horn to call the gods. No sooner had Odin heard the terrible call to arms than he mounted and rode swiftly to Mimer's fountain, that he might know how to lead the gods into battle. When he came, the Norns sat veiled beneath the tree, silent and idle, for their work was done, and Ygdrasil began to quiver as if its very roots had been loosened. What Odin said to Mimer no one will ever know. He had no sooner finished speaking than Heimdal blew a second blast, and out of Asgard the gods rode forth to the last great battle, the golden helmet and shining armour of Odin leading the way. There was a momentary hush as the two armies confronted each other, and then the awful fight began. Shouts of rage rose from the frost-giants, and the armour of the fire-giants fairly broke into blaze as they rushed forward. The Fenris-wolf howled wildly, the hosts of Hel grew dark and horrible with rage, and the Midgard-serpent coiled its scaly length to strike. But before a blow had been struck the shining forms of the gods were seen advancing, and their battle-cry rang strong and clear across the field. Odin and Thor started side by side, but were soon separated. Odin sprang upon the wolf, and after a terrible struggle was devoured. Thor singled out his old enemy, the Midgard-serpent, and in a furious combat slew him; but as the monster died it drew its folds together with a mighty effort and poured upon Thor such a deadly flood of venom that he fell back nine paces, sank down and died. Frey encountered Surt, and because he had not the sword he had given long before to Skirner, could not defend himself, and he too was slain. The dog Garm rushed upon Tyr, the sword-god, and both were killed, Tyr missing the arm which he lost when the Fenris-wolf was bound.

And now the battle was at its height, and over the whole field gods, monsters, and giants were fighting with the energy of despair. Heimdal and Loke met, struggled, and fell together, and Vidar rushed upon the wolf which had devoured Odin, and tore him limb from limb. Then Surt strode into the middle of the armies, and in an awful pause flung a flaming firebrand among the worlds. There was a breathless hush, a sudden rush of air, a deadly heat, and the whole universe burst into blaze. A roaring flame filled all space and devoured all worlds, Ygdrasil fell in ashes, the earth sank beneath the sea. No sun, no moon, no stars, no earth, no Asgard, no Hel, no Jotunheim; gods, giants, monsters, and men all dead! Nothing remained but a vast abyss filled with the moaning seas, and brooded over by a pale, colourless light. Ragnarok, the end of all things, the Twilight of the Gods, had come.

XVII. The New Earth

Ages came and went, and there was no one to count their years as they passed; starless and sunless, the sea rolled and moaned in the great abyss of space. How long that dim twilight lasted no one will ever know, for who, save the All-Father, numbered the ages or kept reckoning of their flight! Invisible, unmoved, the eternal Spirit who had ruled over all things from the beginning, and whose servants the mightiest of the gods had been, kept watch over the starless spaces of the universe, sowing in the measureless furrows the seeds of a new world and a new race.

At last the hour was ripe, and a faint glow stole through the dusky space and spread itself over the sea. It was so dim at first that the waves were hardly coloured by it, but it deepened and deepened until it lay rose-red across the waters, and made all the upper air rich and beautiful. Moment by moment the sky kindled and sent its new glory deep into the heart of the sea, until at last, though there was no song to welcome it, no grateful eyes of men and women to watch its coming, a new sun stood at the threshold of a new day and filled the hollow heavens and the great deep with light and warmth. All day the splendour of the new time bathed air and water in its glow, and when the sun sank at last in the west, and the old darkness began to steal back again, one by one the stars found their places and set their silver lamps swinging in the restless waves.

Day followed day, and night followed night, and yet sun and stars looked down on a wide waste of waters. But there came a day at last when the waters were parted by a point of land, and hour by hour it widened as a new earth rose fresh and beautiful out of the depths of the sea. Over it the sun poured such a glow of warmth that life stirred under every sod; trees shot from the rich soil and made new forests for the wind to play upon; the grass spread itself softly over the barren places, and with deft fingers wove a garment for the whole earth; flowers bloomed along the hillsides and opened their fragrant leaves deep in the forests; birds broke the stillness of the woods and made circles of song in the upper air; the rivers flowed on silently to the sea; the fjords caught once more the shadows of the mountains; and the waterfalls were white with foam of rushing streams.

And when all was ready, and the blue sky once more overarched a world of peace and joy and fruitful fields, Balder came back more fair and beautiful than in the old days at Asgard. With him came his brother Hoder, who had killed him, and they were not long alone; for one by one Hoener, Vidar, and Vale rejoined them. The flame had not touched so much as the hem of their garments, nor had the floods destroyed them. Thor's work was done, but his sons, Magne and Mode, brought back to earth the wonderful hammer which had so often flashed over frost-giants and rung in their ears. More wonderful than all, out of Mimer's forest, where the fountain of memory once stood, and through which the feet of Odin had so often gone in search of knowledge, came Lifthraser and Lif, the one man and woman who had escaped the ruin of the world. And they drank the dew of the morning and grew strong and beautiful. They plucked the sweet new flowers and turned the furrows of the fresh earth, and the harvests waved for them abundantly in all the future years until their children and their children's children filled the whole earth.

The beautiful plain of Ida lay green and bright all the year and bordered with perennial flowers as the suns circled around it; and the gods were at peace at last. No frost-giants invaded the new heaven or darkened the new earth. Through the long bright days Balder and Hoder often sat together and talked of the olden time, of the Midgard-serpent, and the wolf Fenrer, and of Loke's misdoings. Through earth and heaven there was unbroken rest; for often when the gods met to take counsel together the voice of the unseen All-Father spoke to them with infinite wisdom, appeasing quarrels, pronouncing judgment, and establishing peace for ever and ever. And so through all the ages the new world will move to the end. Trees will wave, flowers bloom, stars shine, rivers flow, men toil and reap in the fruitful fields, the gods look lovingly down from the plain of Ida upon their labours; for the hand of the great All-Father will lift men through obedience and industry to himself.